Brady kissed Jane long and hard

A tremor went through her, followed by the first twinges of arousal. After the kiss ended, Jane took a deep breath to steady herself.

"My intention is not to be seduced. Do you understand?"

"Sure, I understand," Brady drawled. "But I don't believe it. Sweetheart, we didn't come to this isolated cottage for the view. That much I do know."

Jane shook her head with exasperation. "You actually think I came here to be seduced?"

"Why not? You're a woman and I'm a man. Women and men do these sorts of things," he said with a teasing laugh. "'Specially in Texas."

"Brady, you're the most confounding man I've ever met!"

"But do I turn you on? That's the question...."

Dear Reader,

By popular demand, Rebels & Rogues returns to Temptation! Over the years we've received lots of positive fan mail about this popular series. You told us how much you *love* stories that focus on the hero—and want more. Well, we've listened. Rebels & Rogues books will appear in the lineup several times a year.

This month's Rebels & Rogues title is written by bestselling author Janice Kaiser, who created an unforgettable hero, Alex Townsend, in the original miniseries. In *The Texan,* you'll meet another great hero by Janice—hunky Texas cowboy Brady Coleman.

Janice and her own hero—and inspiration—husband Ronn, live in sunny California. Among the many interests they share in common is writing, and together they have penned two mainstream novels for MIRA books. Janice is also a regular contributor to Temptation, Superromance and Yours Truly.

Look for a new Rebels & Rogues story soon.

Happy Reading!

Birgit Davis-Todd
Senior Editor, Harlequin Temptation

THE TEXAN
Janice Kaiser

Harlequin Books

TORONTO • NEW YORK • LONDON
AMSTERDAM • PARIS • SYDNEY • HAMBURG
STOCKHOLM • ATHENS • TOKYO • MILAN
MADRID • WARSAW • BUDAPEST • AUCKLAND

To Jack and Susan Pfeiffer

ISBN 0-373-25656-6

THE TEXAN

Copyright © 1995 by Belles-Lettres Inc.

Printed in U.S.A.

Prologue

BY THE TIME THEY crossed the river, the shadows of the big live oaks were growing long in the late-winter sun. At least it wasn't raining, like the year before. It had really stormed then, with two big fronts colliding over south-central Texas. The rain had soaked the parched earth, filling not only the rivers but his sister's freshly dug grave.

Brady Coleman was not happy. He did not want to spend the day taking his mother to the cemetery. Nothing was to be gained from going there. It only made him more angry and more bitter—if that was possible. Besides, much as he loved his mother, he did not particularly admire her stoicism about Leigh's death. There were certain things that couldn't—shouldn't—be accepted, and this, by God, was one.

"I know you're anxious to get this over with, honey," his mother said, "but please, slow down. You know how fast drivin' gets me all jittery."

Without saying a word, Brady eased up on the accelerator. The Lincoln Continental was her car; it was her day. And he'd promised himself he'd do whatever it took to accommodate her—even if it meant driving ten miles an hour under the speed limit. Loretta Channing had her sensitivities like anybody else. He had to recognize that, respect them. Especially on a day like this.

Brady had resolved to play the good son, avoid friction, get through the ordeal without any more words than necessary. He'd put the day and all the emotion it represented behind him. All he had to endure was the visit to the cemetery, dinner, and then it would be over for another year. They could both go back to their lives and not have to struggle over what had happened to Leigh—at least not with each other.

"I was hopin' it'd be easier after another year," his mother said wistfully. "But it isn't."

Brady said nothing. His mother was inviting him into a minefield and he wanted no part of it.

"How about for you, son?" she asked, unwilling to let the subject drop. "Is the pain softenin' any?"

He glanced over at her and saw a sad, somber woman dressed primly in a black wool suit and hat. Her bearing was erect, as always, but he couldn't help but notice how the flowers in her hands shook. "Mama, you see anything to be gained by talkin' about it?"

"I'm still grievin', Brady."

"So am I. But only a fool puts his hand in a buzz saw for no good reason."

"I don't mean to start an argument with you. I just think a body's got to face up to the hurt that's inside them."

"Mama, you can deal with the hurt your way, and I'll deal with it in mine."

He'd speeded up again. When he caught himself doing it, he consciously made himself ease off the accelerator. He was used to driving his battered old pickup hell-bent for leather on the back roads with nobody and nothing to be concerned about but the jackrabbits.

"A family's got to pull together, son," his mother said. "Especially when it comes to things like this. You're all I got anymore in the way of family."

"That's why I'm here," he replied. "That's why I'm taking you to visit Leigh's grave—because it's what you asked me to do."

"I don't want you so full of hate, Brady. All the hate in the world won't bring Leigh back. Comin' to terms with the fact that she's gone is what matters. You've gotta let go! For your own sake!"

"Mama ..."

"Okay, you're right. Sorry I said that. Forget that I did. It's not what you want to hear, I know."

His mother fell silent, but it was too late. Brady's stomach had started churning. His jaw clenched. He felt the adrenaline surging through his veins the same as if it was Jeremy Trent sitting next to him. Hatred, and the desire for revenge, coursed through his blood. It didn't take much to set him off, not when it came to Jeremy. The mere thought of his brother-in-law turned him into a hotheaded young firebrand ready for a barroom brawl.

"Damn it, Mama..." he muttered. It was all he could do to keep from lashing out at her. *Forgetting* was the last thing that was needed. *Remembering* was what was called for. Remembering and never forgetting until his sister's death was avenged!

His mother shifted uncomfortably. "You probably won't like hearin' this much more than what I already said, Brady, but you need a woman in your life. You gave Leigh all your affection and love and never shared a thing with the women in your life. Maybe if you opened your heart to someone new, all the poison in you would drain out."

"Jeez, Mama! Don't we have enough to anguish over already? Besides, being a bachelor's no sin."

"I didn't say it was. You know what I mean, and you know it's true. You just won't admit it!"

"There are more women in my life than I have time for," he said firmly. "I've never wanted for female companionship and you know it. Or are you interested in hearing some of the details?"

"I'm not talkin' about *that* kind of woman, Brady Coleman. I'm talkin' about love, true love with a sweet girl. If you had somebody to devote your affections to, you just might be able to let go of your sister and what happened to her. I know it's none of my business. I know the last thing a man of thirty-five wants is having his mama naggin' him about his love life. And I would not be doing it now, if it wasn't that I can't stand seeing what that hate you're carryin' is doin' to you. It's eatin' at your soul, honey. Don't you see that?"

He forced himself to slow the car again, glancing into the rearview mirror. It seemed every time he came to San Antonio he managed to get a citation. "It's time to change the subject before I say somethin' I'll regret."

"Maybe you just ought to say it and get it over with," she rejoined.

They'd entered the Alamo Heights section of town. Sunset Memorial Park was not far now and his pulse was pounding harder than ever. He was doing his best to fight his anger. "It won't help either of us for me to spout off about Jeremy Trent," he said between his teeth.

"I'm not so sure about that," his mother replied. "Do you ever discuss what you're feelin' with anybody?"

"There's no one I care to discuss it with, unless it's Jeremy himself."

"That's the point I was trying to make. A man needs someone to share the hurts. If he has someone to love, it's easier to let go of the dark side. I know you, Brady. You're the same as your father. Jake could love and hate with a vengeance. And you're the same way, son."

"I don't mean to disappoint you, Mama, but marryin' some poor girl to spare myself trips to the psychiatrist hardly seems a noble thing to do. Besides, much as I respect the females of the species, including you, I don't think their principal mission in life is to save some poor son of a gun from himself. It won't please you to hear this, I know, but I'm satisfied with my life the way it is."

"That's not why I'm suggestin' you settle down, and you know it. I'm tryin' to get you thinkin' positive, to get over your damned obsession with what happened to Leigh."

He paused for a long moment before he spoke. "I can accept her dyin'," he said quietly. "We all go eventually. But I can't accept the sonovabitch who killed her getting away with it—and me being helpless to do anything about it."

"It's not your place to avenge her death, Brady, even if we knew with certainty what happened."

"The hell it isn't! Besides, *I* know what happened."

"You want to believe Jeremy's responsible, but the police don't happen to agree with you."

"They don't have the evidence to convict the bastard, Mama. That's not the same thing. We've discussed all this before. You just don't want to believe Leigh could have made that big of a mistake, marryin' that snake."

"Oh, Brady, don't you see it doesn't make any difference in the long run who did it? I want justice, too, but I'm not going to allow it to eat at my soul and kill me in the process. *Let it go*, honey! Don't burn your life up on what's been a bad enough family tragedy as it is. Please!"

They came to the entrance to Sunset Memorial Park and Brady slowed, swinging the Lincoln into the drive. "You and I see this differently," he said to his mother, "so it's best we leave it at that. It's time now to think of Leigh."

His mother did not argue. She was probably as relieved to end the conversation as he. God knows, it wouldn't be right to stand at his sister's graveside haranguing each other.

They drove past the endless rows of headstones and monuments. He parked by the same mausoleum where the funeral cortege had stopped the February before. The weather could hardly have been more different this time. The sky was clear and a deep blue, as only a Texas sky could be. The air was crisp, but the sun was warm enough. He'd hoped the beautiful day might lighten their spirits, but it seemed his mother was as mired in her passive acceptance of his sister's fate as he was in keeping it alive.

Brady got out of the car, inhaling the fresh, curiously fragrant air. Going around to the passenger door, he helped his mother from the car, taking the flowers from her until she was on her feet. Then she took them back, smoothed her skirt, and they walked side by side to the grave site.

Loretta Channing stood for a minute or two, gazing at the marble headstone. "I'm pleased to see it looks neat and tidy," she said softly. "They do a good job here."

Brady didn't tell her that two days earlier he'd come by the cemetery and given one of the workers twenty bucks to polish the stone and trim the surrounding grass perfectly. His mother cared about appearances, and it was a small enough gesture to assure her peace of mind.

"Would you put the flowers on the grave, son? I'm not sure my back can take the bending."

He placed the flowers as his mother requested, then stepped back to observe the effect. A hush of wind rose, making the blossoms quiver. Loretta took his arm and after a moment began crying softly. His own eyes brimming, he silently gave her his handkerchief.

Brady gazed somberly at the headstone, trying to comprehend that the slab of rock was all that endured of his baby sister, apart from his memories. His eyes passed over her name—Leigh Channing Trent—and that terrible stab of anger welled in him again. It was stronger even than the aching sadness he felt at the loss—so strong that sometimes everything else became a blur. The only thing that gave him any satisfaction at times like this was the thought of his fingers wrapped around Jeremy Trent's neck as he squeezed the life out of the bastard.

A year earlier, as they'd driven away from the cemetery, he'd told his mother he couldn't conscience the thought of the name Trent being tacked onto Leigh's, defiling her headstone. "If it was up to me, I'd take the stone down and put up another with just Leigh Channing on it," he'd said. "I don't care what the bastard thinks."

"Whatever the man did or didn't do, she was his wife, son. That's who she was when she died," Loretta Channing had said. "We have to respect that."

Brady hadn't been persuaded then, nor was he now. Leigh's marriage hadn't been worthy of sanctity. Everybody had known they had problems. Brady had known better than anyone, probably, but the tragedy was that he hadn't fully appreciated the implications of what Leigh was going through.

It still ate at him to know that he might have been able to do something to prevent her death, but he hadn't. He'd been the last family member to talk to her, the last person she'd reached out to. And he had failed her. The guilt he felt over that was almost as bad as the anger at what happened later. A thousand times he'd thought of that final conversation, trying to understand what she'd been trying to say.

In a way, it was surprising how close they'd been. They were half brother and sister; she was nine years younger, still a kid when he was already on his way to college. There had been no love lost between him and her father, Arlo Channing, because the old man had resented him from day one. Their fights were so bad that Arlo had been on the verge of kicking him out when Brady had packed up and headed for A&M to study geology.

Arlo hadn't particularly appreciated Leigh's affection for Brady—or the fact that they shared a mother. Most everybody recognized that Brady Coleman was a free-living rebel like his own daddy, a misfit who'd marched to a different drummer and was more celebrated for his wild living than for anything he'd ever accomplished in life.

And Brady, like his old man before him, was much admired by the ladies. They both were over six feet tall and broad-shouldered, with the same wavy black hair, ice blue eyes and irreverent grin. "Somehow our adventurous Irish soul survived the trip to Texas," Brady's father had once told him in explaining that the Colemans' zest for living had been in the family for generations.

Nobody was surprised when Brady left college before graduation to go into the oil business as a wildcatter, just like his old man. It didn't bother him that Jake Coleman had chased a dream for a lifetime with nothing to show for it in the end. He wound up a penniless dreamer, dying of emphysema in a VA hospital outside Houston.

When he'd gotten back from his father's funeral, Brady had taken Leigh out dancing, saying his father had told him the best way to mourn him was to tie on a good one and kick up his heels with the prettiest gal in Texas. Leigh had always been proud of Brady's admiration. She'd asked him once why he was so attentive to a little sister when half the women in central Texas would have given their eyeteeth to be on his arm. "It's the best way to keep all the predators at bay," he'd told her with a wink. "And I mean to do just that."

Three years later, Leigh was married to Jeremy Trent, the Yankee dandy Brady had loathed from the day he'd first laid eyes on him. And that wasn't just because the bastard had married his little sister. Trent was oily as a skunk and it made Brady sick that Leigh couldn't see through him. If ever there was proof that love was blind, that was it.

Loretta began sobbing more heavily and Brady put his arm around her shoulders, holding her against him. His eyes filled, making his sister's name shimmer on the marble headstone. He bit his lip, coming close to breaking down himself.

"Damn him," he mumbled. "Damn him to hell."

"Don't, honey," his mother sobbed. "Please, Brady."

So he held his tongue. But that didn't keep the tears from running down his cheeks or his anger from welling. He wiped away the tears with the back of his hand, salty, helpless tears that filled him with self-loathing. Standing there, feeling powerless, Brady could hear his sister's plaintive tone the last time they had talked. It was as clear as if she were there beside him now. "Brady, I don't know what to do. I'm at my wit's end. I swear, Jeremy's drivin' me crazy. You've got to help me."

It wasn't like they hadn't talked about Jeremy before. A million times. Brady had always had the same message for her—the son of a bitch didn't belong in the state of Texas, let alone in her bed. The only sensible thing to do was cut her losses, get a divorce. They hadn't had any children, fortunately, so a divorce would have been relatively uncomplicated. It was the best thing she could have done.

But that wasn't what Leigh had wanted to hear. She'd wanted Jeremy to go with her to a counselor, but he'd refused. "I've tried everything," she'd lamented, "but he just won't go."

"Toss him out, for Chrissake!"

"I still care for him, Brady. I love him. That's not the issue. He can be wonderful to me. Absolutely wonderful. It's just at times, he . . ."

"He what?"

She'd sighed with frustration. "The details aren't important. The point is, Jeremy needs professional help and I can't get him to see anybody."

"The professional help he needs begins and ends with some size twelves square in the middle of his backside. I'll kick the bastard out for you, if that's what you want."

"You know it's not. If that's where things were, I'd do it myself. I just thought, bein' a man, you'd have some suggestions on how to persuade him to see somebody who could help him."

"Leigh, it'd help if you'd tell me what's wrong with him. What does he do?"

"It's not important."

"It is if you want me to help. Tell me what he's been doing."

"Oh, just forget it."

"Does he beat you? If he does, I promise I'll rip his goddamn heart out with my bare hands."

Leigh had started crying then.

"Damn," he'd said, "I wish you wouldn't do that."

"I'm sorry I got you from your meeting. I shouldn't have called. I'll just continue doin' what I've been doin'. I'll be as sweet to Jeremy as I can possibly be. Maybe, if he loves me enough, he'll go to a doctor for my sake."

"My advice is better, sugar. Kick his ass out."

Leigh had hung up, sobbing. The next time he saw her she was on a slab in the morgue, having been murdered in her bed. He'd told the police about that call, but they weren't able to link Jeremy to the crime, even though he'd admitted he'd been in their bedroom when she'd died—unconscious, allegedly, while his wife was being murdered by an intruder.

A year had passed. There'd been an extensive investigation with many questions still left unanswered. His little sister and the intruder were both dead. Jeremy was free as a bird, and nobody could prove his story was a damnable lie even though certain things didn't add up.

If only he'd gotten in his truck that day and gone looking for Jeremy. Maybe if he'd banged the sidewinder's head against a wall a few times, Leigh would be alive right now.

His mother was dabbing her eyes. "My little girl," she murmured. Then, stepping around the grave, she approached the stone, placing her hand on it as if she were touching Leigh's silky hair. Tears bubbled from Brady's eyes as he watched.

After a few moments, Loretta Channing left, saying, "I'll be in the car, son, if you want to speak to your sister in private."

Brady started to accompany his mother to the car, but then he stopped. Gazing down at the flowers, he suddenly dropped to his knees and took a deep breath. A sense of calm filled him and he had a strong sense of Leigh's presence. He knew then that there was something that needed to be said. Something that had been in his heart, but never on his lips.

"I love you, Button," he muttered, using his sister's pet name. "And I won't let go of this. I'm going to stay with it until they hang the SOB. He won't get away with it." Brady wiped his eyes and drew an uneven breath. "That's my promise to you, Button. My solemn promise."

1

Three years later

JANE STEWART NERVOUSLY fiddled with her fingers. Over the past few weeks she'd caught herself chewing her nails and biting her lip—things she hadn't done since she was an adolescent. She just wasn't herself.

Even the panoramic view from the window of her "great room," as she liked to call it, was not calming her the way it usually did. She took a deep breath and stared across the water at the lush green of Pebble Beach. The golf course was a magnificent sight, as serene as it was lovely. Yet it had no effect on her.

In the old days, she would come home from a trying day, plop down and absorb the view. Occasionally she'd have a glass of wine to help relax from the rigors of her practice, but normally the healing balm of nature was all it took. That had changed since her accident. No matter how many hours she sat there in her wheelchair, watching as the brilliant hues of late afternoon mutated to softer pastels, that marvelous sense of peace never came to her. Instead she wondered . . . and worried . . . about what lay ahead.

Jane looked down at her body, unused to seeing herself dressed in anything but sweats. Manuela, the housekeeper, had helped her into a pair white silk pants and the white silk-and-angora sweater her sister Margaret had sent her for Christmas. Together they'd put her blond hair up in a French twist, added the beautiful pearl-and-diamond earrings she'd inherited from her mother, and a gold cuff bracelet.

Early on in her recuperation, she'd tried wearing her usual clothes, but doing that soon struck her as a mockery of reality. The fleece outfits she now wore instead were more comfortable and practical. She had them in every color of the rainbow. Her only problem in the morning was to decide if it was going to be a rose day, an amethyst one, or if sea foam or daffodil was more in keeping with her mood.

It was a far cry from life before the accident, when her days were packed with critical, often life-and-death decisions. Now it was what color jogging suit to wear, what to eat for lunch, what to read. Sometimes it seemed like her life was in suspension and there was little she could do but wait for her body to heal.

"Are you okay, Doctor? Is there anything I can bring you?"

Jane turned at the sound of Manuela's voice. The small gray-haired woman of sixty stood at the entrance to the room, a sweet smile on her face, as always. Jane drew a long breath.

"What time is it, Manuela?"

Manuela looked at her watch, turning her wrist to the fading light coming from the windows. "It is twenty minutes before six o'clock," she replied.

"I suppose I have time for a glass of wine before he gets here. Some Chardonnay would be nice."

"*Sí, señorita.*" Manuela pulled the front of her bulky cardigan across her bosom and turned toward the kitchen.

"Just a small one," Jane called after her. "Half a glass."

Manuela left and Jane looked out the window again. She was as anxious as a girl before her first date. That wasn't like her, either.

Manuela returned after a minute with the wine. She paused to switch on a lamp before handing the glass to her. Jane turned her chair to face into the room.

"Thank you."

"You're welcome, Doctor." Manuela stepped back, folding her arms over her chest as she gave her an appraising look.

Jane aimlessly twirled the stem of her wineglass for several moments before taking a sip. Then she glanced at Manuela, who'd been in charge of keeping the house since the day her parents had built it. When Dr. Weldon Stewart died after a sudden illness, two years after his wife had passed on, Jane inherited the place. Manuela had stayed on with her and, after so many years of living in the same house, Jane regarded her as a friend and companion, as well as an employee.

"Do I look as edgy as I feel?" Jane asked.

Manuela smiled. "You look a little pale, *señorita*, but the wine will put color in your cheeks. Don't worry. You look very beautiful tonight. The most beautiful since he is first coming to the house."

"I wish I believed that," Jane said, taking a sip of wine.

"You worry too much, doctor. Señor Trent has admiration for you. Great admiration. It is on his face. Each time a little more. I see it."

"You're just saying that."

"No, *señorita*, it is true."

"It's probably pity. Jeremy is very kindhearted."

"No," Manuela said, shaking her head. "If anybody pities, it is you, Doctor. I have told you this before. You are waiting for your life to come back to you. You are not trying to go to it. This is a mistake."

"Yes, I know, you don't approve." She drank some more wine.

"My approving or not approving is not important," Manuela said. "It only matters that you believe in yourself, as you did before. Your brain is no different. Your face is no different."

"But I'm only half a woman, Manuela. I'm a cripple."

"Forgive me, *señorita*, but this is nonsense. Would you say this thing to a patient? Of course, you would not."

"You're starting to sound like Mark Krinski."

"The doctor, he is right. I agree. Even before he said it to you, I myself think you should be going to your office again. It would be good for you to see the children."

"It would only make me more aware of what I can't do. I can't play at medicine, Manuela. I don't want people making allowances. I'll do my job right or I won't do it at all!"

Her voice had risen, her tone turning caustic. Jane hadn't meant to be sharp. She knew Manuela only had her best interests at heart.

"I'm sorry," Jane said. "I didn't mean to snap." She rubbed the bridge of her nose. "I've been defensive lately. Too quick to criticize. And I'm nervous about tonight."

"Why nervous, Doctor? Señor Trent, he is very kind. And he likes you very much." Manuela sighed. "Before, you didn't have time for the men. All the handsome ones of Monterey, they want to take you out to party, but you are too busy and none of them are so special. And listen to you now, *señorita!* There is no reason for you to be afraid. No reason at all."

Jane turned the glass, spinning the stem between her fingers as Manuela watched her. "Everyone deals with their disabilities in their own way," she said. "Maybe I'm not as brave or strong as some people."

Manuela gave her a disapproving look. "This is nonsense. I have said this to you before, many times. But you are the doctor and me, I am only the housekeeper. Maybe Señor Trent, he will understand you better. I hope so." She gestured toward Jane. "You want some more wine?"

"No, thank you. I only wanted a few sips. Here, you can take the glass back."

Manuela stepped over to take the wineglass. Jane looked at her from under her lashes, feeling the shame of a child. Perhaps sensing her need, Manuela pinched her cheek.

"There, *señorita*, after the wine you have the color of a woman in love. All you need now is to smile, so he will know."

She did smile, but it was an embarrassed smile. "Thank you for caring, Manuela," Jane said, reaching out for her hand.

Manuela took Jane's chin in her hand. "Do you love him? Truly love him?"

"I don't know." Jane looked down at her hands.

"Señor Trent has only been coming here for two months. That is not long."

"Jeremy is kind and understanding. I care for him. But when I try to analyze my feelings, logic tells me I'm needy and insecure right now. That makes me question everything I feel."

"And Señor Trent, what of him? Has he told you his feelings are romantic, *señorita?*"

"No, but I feel they are. He hasn't pressed, ever. I think, out of respect for my condition."

"Señor Trent is a gentleman."

"Yes." Jane sighed.

"Well, I must get back to the kitchen, Doctor, if you are to have your romantic dinner." Manuela patted Jane's hand. "I have told my sister I will be visiting for the night, so I will leave after I serve the dinner and clean the kitchen." She gave Jane a sly smile and left the room.

Jane hadn't told Manuela why she wanted the house to herself that night, but it couldn't have been hard to guess. Of course, Jeremy hadn't signaled that he wanted to make love with her. But he often held her hand or kissed her cheek. He was affectionate. And he cared. She was sure of it.

From the very first, Jeremy had understood her need to face this ordeal on her own terms. When everyone else had pushed her to try harder in physical therapy, to do whatever it took to get on with her life, Jeremy had maintained that some things simply shouldn't be rushed.

For years, she'd been a busy professional, without enough time to stop and smell the roses. She could do that now. She could take the time to appreciate some of the other gifts life had to offer.

Though she knew the advice was sound, implementing it hadn't been easy. She missed practicing medicine. The hours seemed to drag—unless Jeremy was with her. For the first time ever, she had paused to focus on her personal life. And the more she was with

Jeremy, the more she valued his companionship and realized what she'd been missing.

He was understanding and sympathetic. He hadn't once pressed her to make their relationship intimate. That in itself had made her want him all the more. Now she'd reached the point where she wanted to feel like a woman again—a desirable woman.

It had taken a couple of weeks, but finally she'd screwed up her courage to ask if he'd be put off by the notion of a romantic dinner. Jeremy had taken her hand and looked deep into her eyes. And then he'd said, "I can't think of anything I'd enjoy more."

Of course, she wasn't absolutely sure he'd understood what she'd meant—that she wanted them to be alone so he could hold her in his arms, maybe even make love to her. That was why she was so nervous.

Jane heard the grandfather clock in the entry strike six. Trepidation washed over her. Maybe she was being a fool to think that Jeremy might want her. She could hardly blame him if the notion of making love with a cripple was a turnoff.

Jane shut her eyes. Manuela was singing in the kitchen. The sound was strangely reassuring. Jane took a deep breath and told herself she was being silly. Dear God, she had let herself get worked up over nothing . . . again.

If anyone had told her a year ago that she'd be in a funk over the possibility of a romantic dinner, she'd have laughed. Her life had been too full to worry about anything so trivial. The accident had changed that. For the first few hours after a drunk driver had hit her, it wasn't clear if she'd live. Once she was past the critical point and survival was no longer in doubt, the question became whether she'd ever walk again. Would she be able to resume her career, go back to the life she'd had before?

Her doctors were optimistic. Each week her condition looked more and more promising, but one thing was clear—regaining the use of her legs would be a long, slow process. That was a lot to be thankful for. Yet she couldn't seem to focus on the positive. And the longer her recovery period seemed to drag on, the more she felt depressed.

Jeremy had been a godsend. He'd intuitively understood what she was going through. And his quiet words of encouragement were always calculated to put her at ease. She couldn't have picked a better man in her time of need. He was sensitive and compassionate.

Still, she'd resisted any notions of intimacy until she'd checked with Mark Krinski, her orthopedic surgeon. The look on his face had been priceless when she'd asked if it was possible for her to have sex without setting back her recovery.

"Sex . . . ?" he'd said, trying to mask his surprise.

"My libido wasn't crushed, Mark. Only my back."

Once he'd recovered, he'd put his hands on his hips and given her a mock stern look. "I've been wondering how it is I can't get you to leave home to put in a little time practicing again, and here you are, asking for permission to make a circuit of the pickup bars!"

"I'll figure out the who, the how and the when, Mark. I just need you to tell me if it's safe, and what the risks are."

He'd blushed even more than she. "Sorry, Jane. You took me by surprise. I didn't mean to be flip," he'd said, clearing his throat. "Mentally and emotionally, getting involved with life again is the best thing you could do."

"What about physically? You've wanted me to start thinking about exercise. Does this qualify?"

He smiled. "Yes, but you...and your partner... have to use common sense. No rough stuff. If he's gentle and careful you should be all right. Think seven months pregnant."

"Thanks," she said with a wry smile, "but I'd rather not."

He chuckled. "A poor analogy, but you get the point."

"Yes, you're saying I need the right man."

That had been two weeks ago. Now, the moment of truth had come. Jane was listening to Manuela's soft melodic voice warbling in the kitchen when she heard the sound of a car out front. Her stomach tensed. She gave herself a pep talk. Jeremy cared for her, she told herself, so it would work out. It would be just fine, however the evening ended.

A moment later the doorbell rang. She took a deep breath.

"I get it, *señorita!*" Manuela called unnecessarily.

Jane couldn't see the front door from where she sat. The entry was opposite her great room, which was a broad chamber with a two-story vaulted ceiling. Two hemp-colored sofas faced each other in front of a massive, Carmel-stone fireplace. At the far end was the grand piano her mother had so often played in the evenings.

Chairs were scattered here and there, forming separate areas for conversation. The room had been designed for entertaining, and when her parents were alive, it had been the site of numerous festive gatherings. This evening, there was a fire in the huge hearth, giving a feeling of warmth to the space.

Jane heard Manuela opening the front door, and Jeremy greeting her.

"What's that wonderful smell, Manuela? It wouldn't be your cooking, would it?"

"*Sí, señor*. You know very well."

Jane heard the housekeeper laugh. Jeremy was friendly and charming with everyone. She admired him for his thoughtfulness. Everybody who knew him liked him.

Even so, there was a mystery about Jeremy. He was new to the area, having arrived from New England only in the fall. Her introduction to him had come, ironically, through her own family. Her brother-in-law, Peter, had met Jeremy at a Brown University alumni function just before Jeremy was to leave for California. When Peter heard he was planning on settling in the Monterey area, he'd told him he had to look up his sister-in-law.

At first, she'd been annoyed with Peter for having a perfect stranger call her out of the blue, especially considering she was housebound. But Jeremy had seemed so nice on the telephone that she'd invited him over one afternoon for tea. He came again the next week. Soon he was a regular visitor.

Just then Jeremy entered the great room, carrying an enormous bouquet of red roses. He was a good-looking man. His browny-blond hair was medium length and perfectly groomed. He wore a navy blazer with some sort of crest on the pocket, gray trousers, and what looked like a school tie. Jane knew that he'd attended Phillips Academy and Brown—the tie might have been from one of them.

His smile broadened as he approached. Then, when he was ten feet away, he stopped and gazed at her, looking awestruck.

"Jane," he murmured, "you look absolutely beautiful."

"You aren't used to seeing me dressed up, that's all. There was a time when I actually wore normal clothes most days."

He stepped over to her chair and dropped down on one knee, putting the roses in her arms. His soft brown eyes scanned her. "The day will come when you'll wear dresses again and I'll be able to take you on long walks, and I don't mean in your chair."

Jane put her hand to his cheek and smiled. "You're very sweet." She felt a welling of happiness. "And I always thought New Englanders were supposed to be stuffy and cold. How did you get to be such a romantic?"

He took her hand and kissed the backs of her fingers. "It's you, Jane. You're all the inspiration a man needs."

She laughed, seeing that he was teasing her. "Careful. If you lay it on too thick, you'll lose your credibility."

"Hmm. Sweet talk won't do, I see."

Her expression grew serious. "You know, sometimes I do worry that you humor me too much, that maybe I ask for it by behaving like a child."

He shook his head. "Don't be silly."

"I know I've been self-indulgent, that I spend too much time wallowing in my misery."

"Jane, don't talk that way. I have the utmost respect for you and the way you've handled this."

"Why, Jeremy? Why do you feel that way?"

He got to his feet. "If we're going to have a serious discussion, maybe we should go sit by the fire."

"If you like."

He moved behind her wheelchair and pushed her closer to the crackling fire. He sat in a big wing chair next to her and crossed his legs.

"We've gotten to know each other pretty well these past few months," he said. "And the better I know you, the more I respect you. You've gone through an ordeal and you've handled it well—I don't care what you say. Soon you'll be learning how to walk again. You'll need all the moral support you can get and I intend to do my share."

Jane was aware of Jeremy's cologne, a smell that had become familiar. She watched the shadows from the firelight playing on his face. "What if my legs never regain their strength? What if I can't walk again?" she whispered.

"You will."

"But what if I can't? What if I'm in the chair for the rest of my life?"

He leaned forward and took both her hands in his. "Then we'll deal with it, won't we?"

"We?"

"If you'll allow me."

He looked into her eyes with an assurance that made her marvel. How could he be so certain of his feelings when she felt so adrift? She glanced down at the roses.

"Maybe we should get these in a vase," she said.

"Let me take them to the kitchen," he volunteered.

Jane let him have the bouquet and he started off. "Have Manuela put them in the large Waterford," she called after him. "I'd like them on the sideboard in the dining room, too, please."

"All right."

She watched him go, sighing. Once more, Jeremy had calmed her fears. She was still uneasy about what lay ahead, but the immediate tension had dissipated. It was almost as if Jeremy knew what was in her mind—what she needed to hear. Gazing into the fire, she smiled at that thought. Maybe he did. Maybe he knew exactly.

2

JANE LOOKED UP when Jeremy returned. He was carrying an ice bucket filled with champagne, and two glasses.

"Manuela was about to bring this in, so I volunteered, to save her the trip," he said. "Nice idea, by the way."

"It seemed like a festive occasion," she explained.

"It's special because we're together, Jane."

As she watched him open the wine, she wondered what Jeremy was like when he was in a bad mood. No one could be this way all the time. That would be too good to be true.

He glanced at her as he poured the champagne. "What are you thinking?" he asked.

She hesitated. "Nothing special."

"Come now, that was a very contemplative look I saw on your face just now, perhaps even a bit critical. Are you upset about something?"

"Lord, you're a mind reader, too."

He put the bottle back in the ice bucket and handed her one of the glasses. "When you care about someone, you learn to read their moods."

"I see." She wondered why he seemed to be so much better at it than she.

He was back in his chair, his legs crossed, the wineglass in his hand, partway extended. "To a lovely evening," he said, touching his glass to hers.

They sipped their champagne.

"So," he said, "should I be concerned about whatever it is rolling through that pretty head of yours?"

"No, Jeremy." She reached over and touched his hand. "I was just thinking how admirable you are."

"That's hardly need for worry," he said with a laugh.

She studied him. "Have you always been a saint?"

He lifted a brow. "Is that a criticism?"

"Of course not. I'm just trying to understand why you're so good to me."

"The explanation is really very simple." He paused and took a deep breath. "I love you, Jane."

Her heart skipped a beat.

"I fell in love the day we met. Corny as that may seem, it's true." He smiled warmly. "If I'm trying too hard, it's because I can't help myself."

Her eyes suddenly flooded. "What a lovely thing to say," she said, biting her lip, trying to keep from crying. Jeremy leaned over and kissed her. It was a gentle kiss, and by the time it was over, tears were streaming down her cheeks.

"I hope those are tears of joy," he whispered.

She nodded and wiped her cheeks with the backs of her hands, switching her glass back and forth. "Yes, they are."

His face was full of admiration. "Then I couldn't be happier."

"Me, too," she said, sniffling.

He extended his glass toward her. "To the most remarkable woman I've ever known—standing or sitting."

They touched glasses and she took a healthy sip of wine. But her joy was shadowed by an odd feeling of uncertainty. "I wish I *felt* remarkable," she murmured, wanting him to understand her. "The truth is, I feel inadequate...I guess because I haven't been myself since the accident."

Jeremy patted her hand. "You're entitled. God knows, I have my faults. But I love you, which means, if nothing else, that I have impeccable taste." He gave her a teasing smile. "That's my greatest virtue, by the way."

They looked into each other's eyes. "*All* your virtues are obvious," she said. "Tell me about your faults. I want to know everything. The bad along with the good."

He raised his brows in mock dismay. "You're willing to put the evening in jeopardy, eh?"

"I want to hear your darkest secrets." She paused. "If you're willing to tell me."

He looked across the room at the windows and the falling dusk. The lights of nearby homes and buildings were sparkling against the darkening mass of land. From where they sat, the greens were almost indistinguishable from the grays.

"Actually, there is something I've been wanting to tell you," he said, his tone suddenly solemn. "I've got a bit of a past."

The way he said it made her heart drop. "What do you mean, 'a bit of a past'?"

"I was married until very recently, Jane. The divorce wasn't final until four months ago. Just before I came to Carmel."

She was utterly shocked. "Why didn't you tell me before?"

"Because it's a complicated situation. It sounds bad on the surface, and I wanted you to know me well enough to be ready to judge me fairly."

A tremor went through her. "Why do I suddenly feel shaky?"

"Because you're afraid."

"Should I be?"

"Only if you don't trust me."

"Explain, Jeremy," she said. "Please."

"Three years ago I made a very poor decision," he began. "I married a woman I didn't know as well as I should have, nor was I aware of her many problems. She is several years older than I am and has grown children. They resented me from the beginning, though I suppose that is natural enough."

He paused to take a deep breath. "Victoria was addicted to prescription drugs. She had a drinking problem, too. I should have discovered that, but I didn't. She disguised it well. In fact, she gave the impression of being very stable. Underneath she was fragile, living on the edge. And having lost my first wife only a year before, I was more emotionally vulnerable than I realized. I acted impulsively when I asked Victoria to marry me."

"That's hardly a crime," she said. "Everybody makes poor judgments from time to time."

"I'm afraid you haven't heard the worst." His eyes met hers.

Jane swallowed hard and waited.

"A year after our marriage Victoria overdosed on alcohol and barbiturates. She went into a coma and has been in a vegetative state ever since."

"Oh, Jeremy... I'm so sorry."

He looked down at his glass. "Her children blamed me, though of course I had no control over what Victoria did. But I constantly ask myself if I failed her, if there might have been something I could have done to prevent it."

"I would say your worst sin was poor judgment," Jane said. "I can hardly blame you for wanting to end the marriage, given the circumstances. It sounds as though you never had much of a relationship to begin with."

"True. But for better or worse, she was my wife. I didn't want to abandon her, but her children forced the issue. They sued to have the marriage annulled—alleging fraud, all sorts of horrors. It was very ugly." He looked off again at the falling night and sipped his champagne.

"That's terrible. What motivated them to treat you that way? Were they jealous?"

"No, it was greed, pure and simple. Victoria was an exceptionally wealthy woman. I was not without resources, but I had little compared to her. I didn't want her money, but her children did. That's what the fight was really about."

"So what happened?"

"When I realized what they wanted, I decided to swallow my pride and—what was hardest—abandon my wife. I agreed to a divorce and financial settlement that left them the bulk of the estate. My only solace is that Victoria will never know."

Jane shivered, a chill going through her body. She stroked Jeremy's hand. "You have no reason to feel guilty. If anything, what you did was noble, given the circumstances."

He shook his head. "It's wonderful of you to say that, but I can never feel good about what has happened. I might have been able to avoid the whole thing had I been more aware, perhaps more selfless."

"That's silly. You didn't profit from what happened. You suffered."

"But I had no one to blame but myself."

She pressed his hand to her cheek. "You know, despite your positive attitude, I sensed that underneath, something was hurting you. So in a way, this isn't much of a surprise."

"You're more intuitive than I thought," he replied.

"As you said, when you care about someone, you notice things." She smiled.

"Then I haven't disillusioned you?"

"To the contrary, I think more of you than ever."

"And you understand my caution with regard to us," he said. "I haven't pressed because I want to be very sure before...well, moving ahead." He smiled sadly. "First, I wanted to be sure you were strong enough emotionally to have a relationship with me."

"And what have you decided?"

He chuckled. "That if anything, you're the rock, Jane. I have much to learn from you."

"That's not true, but thank you for saying it." She drained the last of her champagne and Jeremy took the bottle from the ice bucket and refilled their glasses. Then he tossed another log on the fire. Jane watched the flames envelop the wood and listened to the crackling of the fire. Then she glanced at Jeremy, who was watching her intently.

"There is something I want now that I didn't want before," she said, her voice almost somber. "And I've worried about how to tell you."

"What is it, Jane?"

She gazed at the fire again, unable to look into his eyes. "I need to be treated as a woman, not as an invalid who must be coddled."

Jeremy's brow furrowed. "I'm not sure I understand."

She bit her lip, but still didn't look at him. There was a loud pop in the fireplace. A train of sparks rose, disappearing quickly from sight. "I'd like for you . . . to . . . make love with me," she whispered.

Jane did look at him then, to see his reaction. His eyes glistened. He leaned across her chair and kissed her. It was a deeper, more passionate kiss. "I love you, Jane," he murmured.

She assumed that meant yes, but she wasn't sure. She gazed into his eyes. Jeremy touched her face.

"Can you?" he asked.

"My doctor said I could if I was careful. You'd have to be gentle. But I don't want you to do it if you don't want to . . . if the idea repulses you, I mean."

"Don't be silly." He kissed her again.

"Manuela is going to her sister's for the night," she said.

A quirky grin spread across his mouth. "You're a regular seductress, aren't you?"

"I care for you, Jeremy. Very much."

He held both her hands and stared into her eyes for a long time. Then he took her champagne glass from her and put it and his on the table beside his chair. Clearing his throat he said, "I was going to wait until after dinner, but now may be the time to do this." He reached his hand into his pocket and pulled out a velvet box. "It's probably premature, and maybe unfair of me to broach the subject when you've got so much to deal with, but I want you to know my intentions."

He popped open the box then. There was a large square-cut diamond inside, a huge stone. "I want you to marry me," he said, his voice thick with emotion.

Jane swallowed hard, disbelieving.

Looking into her startled eyes, he added, "I don't expect an answer now. But I'd like for you to play with the idea, see how it feels."

Jane shook her head, stunned. "Jeremy, I'm . . . speechless."

"I know I haven't so much as hinted at this, but I simply couldn't wait." He slipped the ring on her finger. "Wear it during dinner, at least. If you don't want to keep it on after that, I'll understand."

She shook her head again. Her mind was spinning. "I don't know what to say. I knew you cared, but . . ."

Jeremy shrugged, smiling. "You see, I can be unpredictable. I hope that's all right with you."

She looked down at the ring. "It's more than all right."

"Then you're not unhappy."

"No, of course not." She hesitated. "It's just that this is so unbelievable."

"You'll find I'm a man of many surprises." He took her hand and together they gazed at the ring.

She couldn't tell him, but this wasn't the sort of complication she'd have chosen. Marriage had always seemed like something she would face way down the line. But there was one good thing—she didn't have to wonder about his intentions anymore. Jeremy had put his feelings on the line.

THE AIR COMING IN the window was cool on his bare skin. It felt good. Her fingers skittering across his chest felt pretty good, too. When Brady began purring like an old mountain lion, Laureline ran her hand down his body to his loins, taking him in her hand. After she'd caressed him for a while, he smiled.

"Surely you're not sayin' you want more, darlin'," he said, his voice throaty.

She rolled her head on his chest, kissing his skin with the corner of her mouth. "Brady, honey, I al-ways want more of you. Besides, I didn't drive a hundred miles tonight for a wham-bang-thank-you-ma'am."

"Is that what you call it? I'd say it was one of my better performances."

"Too good, honey," she replied. "I'm still buzzin'."

He tousled Laureline's ebony curls, holding her head to his chest. She wrapped her thigh around his leg as he looked out the window at the night sky.

Brady could see the Milky Way—thousands and thousands of stars—and a fat slice of moon. The crystal-clear air was one of the things he appreciated most about Edwards Plateau country—that and the vast emptiness of it. There were millions of acres of rolling limestone hills, cut by wide arid canyons and sprinkled with live oak, juniper, piñon pine and even pecan trees near the water in the bottoms.

His two thousand acres bordered Pulliam Creek, most of it on the bluff. The land had little commercial value—a neighbor ran cattle on part of it. There was a marginal gas well that brought in enough to pay the taxes and the insurance on the property, with enough left over for a night on the town in Dallas or Houston or New Orleans. But he didn't keep the place for economic reasons. He kept it because of its beauty, because of the deer that came down from the hills in the morning, the quail, the arid winds of summer and the frosty gales of winter.

The ranch was his place of refuge where he could read by the fire. He loved books. He had over three thousand volumes—more than many small libraries. His collection covered nearly every subject, although he especially liked biographies, anthropology and natural history.

At the moment Laureline was doing her best to turn him on. She swirled her tongue around his nipple, sending twinges through his spent body. She was one of those rare women who was overtly sexual, yet not cheap. And when she wanted sex, she got her way... always. He'd found out the hard way how difficult it was to say no to her.

Laureline was the ex-wife of his best friend, Jerry Branson. When she'd finally divorced her philandering husband, she'd come after him with a vengeance. "Don't know why I didn't marry you to begin with instead of Jerry," she'd once said. "You're twice the man."

Brady, with his usual no-holds-barred brand of honesty, had replied, "Probably because he asked you, sugar, and I didn't."

Laureline hadn't liked that, but she knew him well enough to know he wasn't the type to tell a woman he loved her if it wasn't true. He'd charm a girl if it served his purposes. He'd hedge and he'd evade. But it was his code never to outright lie.

Over the past several weeks he'd been doing his best to let Laureline know that mercy sex was one thing, but anything more serious was another matter altogether. He'd thought he'd be safe at the ranch—given the distance from San Antonio. But she'd shown up on his doorstep at dusk wearing a tight skirt and knee-high Italian boots, her hormones throbbing.

Brady groaned, knowing a man could have worse problems.

"What's the matter, honey?" Laureline asked. "Am I keeping you up?"

"No, darlin', I was expecting a call. That's all."

"At this time of night? It's after ten."

"From California."

She lifted her head from his chest and looked at him in the faint light. "Who'd be callin' from California? Is it a woman?"

"No, it's a detective, if you must know. A man out of Austin doing a job for me."

"Oh." She rolled back against him, giving him a kiss of contrition on the shoulder. "It's about Leigh, isn't it?"

He drew a long breath. "Yep."

"You're obsessed with her bein' murdered, aren't you?"

"I'm obsessed with seein' the bastard who did it hung, if that's what you mean."

"I don't mean to tell you your business, Brady, but what good's it doin' to hang on like you are? Even Jerry said it's eatin' at you like a cancer."

"Laureline, the bastard's a predator. He's already tried to kill his second wife back in Connecticut and now he's off huntin' for a third out in California. I took some of the money I got sellin' those leases I had down in Zavala County and hired this guy to see exactly what J.T.'s up to."

"What good's that goin' to do?"

"If I can spare another family the grief ours and the folks in Connecticut have gone through, then I will. And if I make his life miserable in the process, so much the better."

"It's your money," Laureline said, "and your life. But I sure hate seein' what it does to you. You aren't the same person when you get to talkin' about J.T. and Leigh."

"I'm sorry if that upsets you, but a man's got to do what a man's got to do."

He began running his hand over the soft skin of her belly then, half deciding he wouldn't be getting his call anyway. The truth was, Laureline was right. He was in the grip of something that just wouldn't let go. He had to keep going until he killed it, or it killed him. There seemed to be no other way.

"It's a real shame you feel that way, Brady, because it's ruinin' your life. Of course, it wouldn't matter if you weren't so good in the sack," Laureline said wistfully.

He laughed.

"It's not funny," she protested, giving him a jab in the stomach.

"I didn't say it was." He tried to keep a straight face, but was having a hard time.

Laureline propped herself up on one arm and looked him dead in the eye. "Damn it all, anyway. I hate men, Brady. Honest to God, I do. I hate y'all." She took a deep breath and sighed. "I wasn't going to tell you till the mornin', but I've decided to leave San Antonio."

Her comment brought him up short. "To go where?"

"I don't know. Houston. New Orleans. Someplace. I need to start over."

He felt a twinge in his gut. Guilt. Sadness, too. "I understand."

"You don't, but that's okay."

"I hope I haven't disappointed you too bad, Laureline."

"Of course you've disappointed me, you dumb lug. But I don't blame you. You never lied to me or made promises. Not like Jerry."

He patted her leg. "Don't let the likes of me and Jerry spoil things for you, Laureline. There's a fella out there who deserves you, believe me."

For an answer, she began crying softly. Brady gathered her close and stroked her head. He'd have liked nothing better than to love her. But his feelings for women never seemed to run that way. His mother and Leigh were the only exceptions, and the love he felt for them was entirely different.

Before he died, his old man had told him that he'd either loved every woman he ever met or else he never loved a one—it was hard to tell which. Brady had come to understand that, but it hadn't been a very reassuring notion.

The phone on the nightstand rang, making him jump. "That's my call. Excuse me, darlin'," Brady said, pulling from her embrace. He reached for the phone. "Coleman."

"Mr. Coleman, this is Warren Nuckhols. Sorry to call so late."

"No problem, Warren. What do you have?"

"Took me a while, but I found our man in Monterey, down the coast from Frisco. He's settled in and is already on the scent."

"You mean he's got a woman lined up?"

"Yes, sir. It appears they're already seriously involved."

Brady shook his head, feeling both disgusted and sick at the same time. "Well, it seems ol' J.T.'s talents are improving with practice. What's this one like, Warren?"

"Rich, as you might guess. The lady has a lot of family money. Megabucks. And she's a doctor. Name's Jane Stewart."

"That's a surprise. I'd have thought a professional would have more sense. Is she old? A widow?"

"No, sir. She's thirtyish. Never married. Really quite attractive. I saw a picture of her in the hospital directory. She's a big step up from the lady in Connecticut."

"How does he fool 'em, Warren?" Brady asked with disgust.

"Smooth as snake oil, I suppose. God, if I knew his secret I wouldn't be spending my time playing detective."

"I don't know why I'm so surprised. I saw the SOB with my sister. Leigh was no fool, but she couldn't see through him. I guess he knows how to spot a weakness and take advantage."

"It's not hard to guess what this Jane Stewart's weakness is, Mr. Coleman. She's in a wheelchair, if you can believe it."

"Oh, God. She's handicapped?"

"I haven't gotten the particulars, but she's housebound. She isn't practicing medicine, that's for sure. That's the main reason I haven't gotten a good look at her."

Brady rubbed his chin. "Keep digging, Warren. Find out everything you can without raising suspicion. Maybe it's time for me to hop on a plane and check things out firsthand."

"I wouldn't wait long," Nuckhols said. "He married the heiress in Connecticut three months after they met. Near as I can tell, he's almost put in that much time with this one. And you can bet he's serious. He's already got her a ring."

"How'd you find that out?"

"Tailed him for three or four days, to see how he's living. Before he went to her place last night, he stopped by a jewelry store."

"Great."

"And he didn't leave her place until this morning."

"Wonderful. He's making it with a paraplegic."

"Couldn't tell you about that."

"That's okay, Warren, I don't need details from the bedroom."

"For what it's worth, Mr. Coleman, our boy spent this afternoon in San Francisco with a call girl. Drove up from Monterey after leaving the doc's place."

"Maybe he didn't get any, after all."

"Or could be he likes variety."

Brady sighed. "I can hardly be critical of that."

"But he does have the bad habit of turning wives into corpses," Warren Nuckhols added.

"Yeah, a very bad habit. One I'd like to break him of."

3

FLYING WEST GOT HIM into San Francisco at a fairly decent hour, though the weather wasn't much to shout about. It was a gray, rainy evening and he'd seen nothing but clouds on their approach—no lights, no bridges, no picture-postcard views. Brady asked the Chinese doll at the car-rental desk about likely traffic conditions between the airport and Monterey and she told him he'd have to fight the rush-hour snarl all the way down the peninsula and through San Jose.

"What's a cowboy who hates traffic to do?" he asked, giving her a sly grin.

"If it was me, I'd kill some time here at the airport and set out later," she said. "Have an early dinner."

"Any recommendations?"

She told him where she usually ate.

"Your dinner break coming up soon?"

The girl smiled. "My husband won't let me eat with strangers."

Brady looked at her ringless finger. "Smart fellow. Does he know you take off your ring every time you leave the house?"

"I'm allergic to metal. Can't wear jewelry."

He gave her a wry look. "Ah, every man's dream."

"Enjoy your dinner, Mr. Coleman," she said, giving him the rental documents and an endearing smile.

Brady winked and went off to find a place to eat.

He wound up with a poor excuse for a steak, but he made do. After gathering his luggage from the locker where he'd stored it, he went in the rental-car bus to pick up his wheels. The clerk who handled his paperwork was also Asian, but a male this time. He showed Brady the route to Monterey on the map. Once on the freeway it was a straight shot seventy-five miles south, a little less than the distance from San Antonio to Austin.

The going was slow through San Jose, though he was on the tail end of the rush hour. It rained sporadically, which meant he had to keep turning the wipers on. The darkness prevented him from seeing much. As nearly as he could tell, northern California wasn't all that different from southern California, which was the only part of the state he knew.

As was usual when he spent much time alone— whether it was behind the wheel of his pickup, or riding horseback on the buttes above Pulliam Creek— Brady started thinking about Jeremy. The mental image of the bastard's smug face was more than enough to set the blood pounding in his temples. Sometimes, the thought of Jeremy would make his breath grow short and he'd feel a terrible pressure in his chest.

Brady knew he couldn't think about the bastard incessantly, but it was hard not to. Sometimes, the only way he could get him out of his mind was to play tricks on himself. The company of a woman helped. When that wasn't possible, he'd think about the past, about the days before Leigh's death.

This time, he concentrated on his memories of California. Five years earlier he'd flown out to negotiate an oil lease with Harley Orman, a former Texan living in Newport Beach. While in L.A. Brady had driven around in the smog, checking out the palm trees and the young girls in flashy convertibles. He'd driven to Malibu one afternoon to have a look at the J. Paul Getty Museum—Greek and Roman art fascinated him. But the highlight of the trip had come after the negotiation was completed. Harley had lined up a couple of girls and the four of them had gone over to Vegas to blow off steam. Brady won five grand at the crap tables, gave Tammy—or whatever her name was—half since she'd thrown the dice for him, and yet still managed to cover the expenses of the trip.

Northern California was supposed to be a different sort of place, but in the rain and dark he couldn't say how. He pulled off the freeway at a place called Morgan Hill and bought a cup of coffee at McDonald's. Sitting by a blackened window streaked with rain, he watched a Mexican family of six eating burgers and milk shakes. It made him think of the babies Leigh might have had if she'd married Tommy Bradshaw or one of the other boys who'd been in love with her. He'd be the uncle of two or three giggling little girls or boys right now. Instead, he was a couple of thousand miles from home, full of sorrow and hate, and on the trail of the bastard who'd killed his sister.

To anybody else, that probably seemed crazy. He'd left his nice cozy ranch to go off tilting at windmills, trying to save the butt of a woman who probably had no desire to be saved. Leigh hadn't listened to him. What made him think a perfect stranger would?

But in his heart, he knew this really wasn't about a beautiful doctor in a wheelchair. It was about a man who preyed on innocent women, a man who had to be brought to justice. And in a way it was about Brady's own failures, too—his inability to save Leigh. If that wasn't worth selling off some potentially lucrative oil leases, what was? What good was money if a man had no self-respect?

Brady finished his coffee and continued on his rainy drive, fighting his devils, his jaw clenched. He arrived in Monterey around nine-thirty and found Warren Nuckhols's motel.

Getting out of the car, he smelled the ocean for the first time. He took a couple of deep breaths, hoping for an omen, some sign that this would be the place of decision.

Nothing came to him. All he could say was California sure didn't smell like home. No, this sure as hell wasn't Texas. But was it the place where old scores would be settled, where he'd see justice done? There was no way to know. Yet, with a little luck, California might prove to be the end of the trail for Jeremy Trent. That was what he'd been living for. He sure as hell wasn't going to let this opportunity slip away. Not without the fight of his life.

JANE SAT AT THE TABLE in the breakfast room, nibbling toast as she listened to a Beethoven piano sonata. She found herself constantly looking down at the diamond on her finger. She must have glanced at it a thousand times since Jeremy had given it to her.

Jeremy had been right when he'd said it was premature. But he'd also said he didn't expect an answer—he only wanted her to think about it. It was a clever strategy. She'd done little else. Jeremy had stayed the night, but he hadn't made love with her. He'd simply held her. That had been clever, too. It had made her desire for him all the more poignant.

His love was proving to be a tonic. Yet she hadn't embraced the notion of marriage. Why? For a long while after Jeremy had fallen asleep she'd lain there, running their short history through her mind.

Jeremy had understood her, right from the start. He was intelligent. An excellent conversationalist. But it was the uncanny way he identified her vulnerabilities and addressed her emotional needs that really got to her.

Jeremy knew how to play on a woman's curiosity, as well. He had an air of mystery that added to his charm. Some women might have been put off by that, but she liked it. In truth, if anything about him gave her pause it was the fact that she hadn't figured out what motivated him.

If Jeremy Trent had dreams, he didn't discuss them. She only had a vague impression of what he did for a living. He'd spoken of a family trust. Otherwise he hadn't said much about that aspect of his life, either. And she hadn't questioned him because she felt it wasn't any of her business.

As far as she could tell, Jeremy's interests tended to be more social than financial. When he'd expressed a desire to get involved with the local hospital charity, she'd put him in touch with Marian Montross, the committee chair. Marian had introduced him around and she said he'd already become active, although Jeremy himself had said nothing of that to her, leading her to believe he was modest as well as enigmatic.

Peter hadn't told her anything about Jeremy's life, either, but she sensed the social scene was important to him. While it wasn't a major part of her life, Jane was at home in "society." The Stewart name meant automatic entry into almost any social gathering.

Her grandmother, Elsa Stewart, had been the grande dame of Monterey society in the twenties and thirties. Her connections ran from the parlors of Pacific Heights and Russian Hill in San Francisco to the Hearsts in San Simeon. Elsa had dined with Hollywood luminaries as well as industrial scions.

Jane's parents had lived a much quieter life, centered around Pebble Beach and the country-club set. They were active in charitable causes and were well respected. The Stewart name still held a certain cachet, which to her was a burden as well as a benefit. What she didn't know was how important that name was to Jeremy.

Since he'd given her the ring, Jane couldn't help wondering what they'd be like as a couple. Having a charming husband was not a bad thing for a woman committed to a career. The reverse had worked well for centuries. Maybe Jeremy was just what she needed.

Jane sipped her coffee. Outside, the sun continued to burn off the fog. Manuela was humming in the kitchen. Once she had finished the dishes, she would head for Gilroy to visit her sister. In the past they'd arranged for a day nurse whenever Manuela was away for more than a few hours. But Jane was strong enough now, that that wasn't necessary.

She wouldn't be seeing Jeremy, either. He'd headed to San Francisco, saying that from there he'd be flying east to meet with his lawyer. He wouldn't be back for two or three days.

In a way she was glad for the respite. She wanted to get some perspective on his proposal. She already knew she wouldn't give him a quick answer. She'd hinted she might not be ready to make a decision until she was on her feet again. "I want to meet you on equal terms," she'd told him, even knowing that the extent of her recovery remained in doubt.

"So, Doctor, you need anything before I go?" Manuela was standing in the doorway, wiping her hands on a tea towel.

"No, Manuela, I'm fine. You go ahead and enjoy your day."

"Where do you want to be?" she asked. "You want that I take you to the big room? Or maybe your bedroom."

"I'm fine. I can manage now, Manuela. Really. Just go."

"You have your portable telephone?"

Jane looked down at the empty hook on the arm of her chair. "No, I forgot it."

"You wait, *señorita*, I get it for you."

Manuela left to get the phone. When she returned, she gave it to Jane and then said goodbye. Minutes later, Jane heard her going out the back door. Then there was the rumble of Manuela's bad muffler as the car headed off. The house fell silent. Even Beethoven had forsaken her. Jane wheeled into the great room, trying to decide if she wanted more music, or if she'd go with the silence for a while.

She looked out at her view. The fog had almost completely dissipated, but the wind had come up, bringing in broken clouds from the Pacific. It was one of those unpredictable days. For several minutes she watched the surf pounding the rocks, but soon discovered she was restless. Her introspective life was beginning to wear.

Just then the doorbell rang. Her first thought was that Manuela had forgotten something. But she wouldn't ring the bell. Jeremy was in Connecticut. Her friends wouldn't drop by without calling. It wouldn't have been polite.

The bell rang a second time and Jane decided to ignore it. Because hers was a gated community, few solicitors made it in. And neighbors didn't drop in, not in Pebble Beach. Whatever it was, she was in no mood for uninvited guests.

When the bell rang a third time her curiosity was really aroused. If it was a burglar checking to see if the house was occupied, she'd be wise to let him know it was. Jane wheeled over to the entry, arriving as the bell sounded a fourth time. The peephole was too high to be used from her chair, leaving her no option but to talk through the door.

"Who is it?" she called out firmly.

There was no response for a moment, then she heard a man's voice drawl out, "Brady Coleman. I'm here to see Jane Stewart."

"Do I know you, Mr. Coleman?"

"No, ma'am, but you should."

She frowned. "What do you want?"

"To talk."

"Well, I'm afraid I'm indisposed at the moment."

"Ma'am?"

"I can't see you now, Mr. Coleman," she said more loudly. "I'm not in the habit of opening the door to strangers."

"Maybe I should have called first," he said, showing no sign of giving up.

The accent was Southern. She couldn't imagine who he was or what on earth he wanted, but she wasn't going to open the door to find out. "That would've been the polite thing to do," she said firmly. "You might have explained what you wish to talk about."

"I would have, but there's a problem, Miss Stewart. I don't know your number. It's unlisted."

Jane rolled her eyes. She had half a mind to call the police and have the man removed from her doorstep. Instead she gave him the number, thinking the worst that would happen was that he'd phone.

"Thank you," the unseen Mr. Coleman said through the door. "You have a nice day now."

Jane turned her chair around and was just leaving the entry when the portable phone rang. She answered it. "Hello?"

"Brady Coleman, ma'am" came the reply. "Hope I'm not disturbing you."

She looked back at the front door, astonished. "Weren't you just...wasn't I talking to...the same Mr. Coleman who was just at my door?"

"Yes, Miss Stewart."

"How..."

"Cellular phone." He chuckled. "The wonders of modern technology. I guess the connection's a little better than when we were talkin' through the door."

"Mr. Coleman, what do you want? I don't have time for games. If you're a solicitor, I don't intend to talk to you."

"I'm not a solicitor. As a matter of fact, I flew in last night from San Antonio just to talk to you."

"About what?"

"I hesitate to put it in these terms, but it's accurate enough—about life and death, ma'am. *Your* life and death."

Jane looked at the phone and then at the door, wondering what kind of nut she was dealing with. "Is this some kind of a joke?" she demanded. "Just who are you?"

"Jeremy Trent's former brother-in-law," Coleman replied. "At least, I was until my sister was killed and he hightailed it off to Connecticut. That's who I've come to talk to you about—J.T."

Jane's heart skipped a beat. Then she pulled herself together and rolled her chair to the door. She turned the dead bolt and swung the door open.

He was standing on the second step, one booted foot resting on the top one, the cellular phone still to his ear. Seeing her, he clicked the instrument off and slipped it into his pocket. He looked her over, a slow, languorous grin spreading across his face.

Brady Coleman was wearing a sheepskin coat. His dark jeans hugged his legs, running down over his alligator-skin Western boots. All that was missing to make the image complete was the Stetson.

His grin turned roguish as he saluted her. "Morning, Miss Stewart. I appreciate you seeing me on such short notice."

Jane was in no mood for affability. "What's this about Jeremy and your sister?"

Coleman's expression turned sober. "Don't tell me ol' J.T. omitted mentioning he was a widower. That his first wife was killed under mysterious circumstances—in their own bed."

"I was aware his first wife had died tragically, but—"

"Oh, it was tragic, all right. She was murdered."

Brady Coleman was giving her a hard, level stare. The easy amiability was gone. Jane blinked. "You're serious."

"Dead serious, ma'am."

She was at a total loss. There was obviously a point to this, but she didn't know what. "You aren't suggesting Jeremy was responsible, are you?"

"What did *he* tell you about her death?"

"Nothing, really. I assumed it was an accident."

"It wasn't."

Jane gazed at him, dumbfounded. What she was hearing wasn't registering clearly. It seemed insane. A bad joke.

"You were aware that J.T.'s second wife is now in a coma after having been given an overdose of drugs, I suppose."

"I knew she had an addiction problem and that she overdosed on alcohol and drugs, yes," Jane said uneasily. "Jeremy's told me all about the unfortunate incident."

"*All* about it?" Coleman said incredulously. "Somehow I doubt that."

On one level, his sarcasm annoyed her, although she couldn't help but be distressed by what he was actually saying. "If you've come here to accuse Jeremy of wrongdoing, Mr. Coleman," she stammered, "then you ought to be honorable enough to say whatever you have to say to his face."

"Oh, J.T. knows what I think of him. He's heard it before. There's nothing shy about me, Miss Stewart, I assure you."

Jane clasped her trembling hands. "No, evidently not."

Although the entry to the house was protected from the wind, the air was chilly. Shivering, she began rubbing her arms.

"I can see you're cold," he said. "Do you trust me enough to let me step inside, so you can be comfortable while we talk?"

"I don't know that there's any more we have to say to each other, Mr. Coleman. If you have a problem with Jeremy, it's none of my affair."

"I beg to differ, ma'am. The reason I'm here is to warn you of what you're up against. J.T.'s given you his version of his life story, I'm sure. It's only fair you hear me out."

"I know everything I need to know."

"How can you be so sure?"

She rubbed her arms again, as much from anxiety as from cold. "Do I look like a fool?"

"All due respect, ma'am. My sister wasn't a fool, but she was taken in by him. And so was the woman in Connecticut."

Jane bristled. He was suggesting she'd been conned and she didn't like that one little bit. But the look on his face said he wasn't about to be dismissed. Still, he was making outrageous accusations. A total stranger. If anyone was the con, it was more likely he.

"Thanks for your concern, Mr. Coleman," she said, gathering herself. "But I see no need for further discussion. I'll talk with Jeremy about this when I see him. Now, if you'll excuse me . . ." She started to back out of the doorway.

"Jane," Brady Coleman called to her with distinct urgency, "you owe it to yourself to hear me out. After I've had my say, I'll leave. Regardless of what you think of me, you ought to at least listen."

"It isn't necessary."

"Are you afraid of what you might hear?"

"Of course not," she snapped.

"Then what have you got to lose by inviting me in? If I was up to no good, I'd already have done it."

"Seems to me you already have."

He gave her a lazy smile. "What I've said is only the tip of the iceberg."

She shivered again. The logical thing was to close the door and be done with it. But the man's combination of insistence and sincerity gave her pause. "Well, step inside, out of the cold," she said. "But only for a minute."

4

JANE BACKED HER wheelchair from the door to give him room to get by her. "But when I ask you to leave, Mr. Coleman, I expect you to go," she said.

He nodded solemnly. "Ma'am, I may talk with a drawl and wear jeans, but I'm a gentleman. If it helps, I'm here for the sake of my sister, Leigh, not for myself."

"All right, come in."

As she watched, Brady Coleman stepped inside. Now that they were on the same level, he appeared even larger than he had when standing on the stairs. She was sure he was at least six-three. He closed the door carefully, as though he were leaving the room of a sleeping child, then rewarded her with an amiable grin.

Glancing around, he said, "Nice place you have here, Miss Stewart." His intent obviously was to put her at ease. "Or should I address you as Dr. Stewart?"

"You called me Jane once," she answered. "No sense standing on ceremony now."

"When I'm earnest I sometimes get familiar," he said by way of apology. "Please forgive me."

"No apology required, Mr. Coleman."

"Brady will do."

"All right. Brady, please say what you wish to say. But you may as well know I don't feel the least bit comfortable about this."

"I'm sure it's not easy having some stranger walk into your house and begin bad-mouthing your fiancé."

"You seem to know a lot about me and Jeremy. How is that?"

"I've had a private investigator on J.T.'s tail for years, off and on. I'm in the oil business and whenever the good Lord sees fit to bestow a bit of America's bounty on me, I use some of the money to see what Jeremy's up to. It's become an obsession, as you might have guessed."

"Apparently so."

Brady Coleman unbuttoned his coat, revealing a red plaid wool shirt and a large silver belt buckle. He was ruggedly handsome, with wavy black hair, incredible blue eyes and a strong jaw—everything she'd once imagined a cowboy to be, and then some.

"Will what you have to say take long?" she asked.

"Depends whether I give you the five-dollar or the twenty-dollar version."

"Let's say the five-dollar version."

He shrugged. "Fifteen, twenty minutes."

Jane looked at her watch to signal her time was not without limits. "Why don't you take off your coat and we can go in and sit down?"

She turned her chair and headed for the great room. Brady came up behind her.

"Can I give you a hand?"

"Thank you, but I'm trying to be self-sufficient."

He took the handles of the chair anyway and proceeded to push her. "Sorry, but it's not my nature to watch a lady struggle with anything."

"You *are* a gentleman," she said, glancing over her shoulder.

"It's the flip side of being a male chauvinist, I guess."

"Are you a male chauvinist, too?"

He stopped in the middle of the great room and stepped around to where she could see him. He stroked his chin. "If I said no, you wouldn't believe me. If I said yes, you'd probably figure I was arrogant and proud of it. The best thing, I think, is to let you judge for yourself."

He slipped off his coat, tossed it on the nearest chair, and strode to the picture window. "Mind if I take a minute to admire your view? That's where they play the Crosby, isn't it?"

"They don't call it that anymore, but yes."

"You play golf, Jane?" He glanced back at her. "I mean, before you landed in that chair."

"Not really. Having played a few rounds doesn't make a person a golfer, I'm told."

"I don't play, either," he said, peering at the view again.

His hands were on his hips, his broad shoulders and narrow waist silhouetted against the morning light. Rough-hewn or not, the man had a physical appeal that couldn't be denied.

"Livin' in the Hill Country, a fella's more likely to shoot jackrabbit or deer than knock a little ball around a big lawn." As soon as he said it, he turned around. "Or is it politically incorrect of me to mention hunting? You aren't an animal-rights type, are you?"

"I'm not an activist, if that's what you mean. But I don't support the slaughter of animals for sport, either."

Brady winced. "I woke up this mornin' remindin' myself I was in California and I had to watch my mouth. So what do I do right off, but mention hunting."

"I won't get emotional about it, Brady, so don't worry."

He meandered to a chair and dropped into it. "For what it's worth, I never shoot anything I won't eat." Then he steepled his fingers as he regarded her, his affability evaporating. "Forgive the personal question, Jane, but are you permanently disabled? My man wasn't sure."

"Your man?"

"The detective I hired. His name is Nuckhols."

She stared at Brady Coleman, trying to decide about him. "You know, I think I should be offended."

"You *think* you should?"

"You come to my house and tell me you've been investigating me and my...my..." She looked down at her finger and turned the ring around it. "My friend."

He grinned. "I thought that was an engagement ring. Didn't J.T. give it to you a couple nights ago, before heading off to Frisco?"

She bristled. "You *have* been snooping! You've invaded my privacy," she said. "And frankly, I'm offended. Extremely offended!"

"Sorry, I meant no offense."

"What do you mean, you meant no offense? You tell me you've had somebody snooping on me and all but accuse the man I...I...feel very deeply for...of being a murderer. How do you expect me to feel?"

"Whoa, hang on a second. My man was watching J.T., not you. I'm here because I wanted you to have the whole story before you married the SOB. And I'm doing this at no small sacrifice, by the way. It's purely a humanitarian gesture."

"Maybe I'm not interested in being saved," she retorted, still annoyed.

"You can't be stupid," he said. "Are you stubborn?"

"Look, mister, I don't know you from Adam. You're accusing a man I respect of God-knows-what. Then you have the nerve to suggest I'm stubborn when I don't embrace you with open arms! Well, maybe I *am* stubborn. But you, you've got gall!"

Brady Coleman squeezed the bridge of his nose as if he had one heck of a headache. "You're right," he said. "I was out of line. It's just that every time I think of Leigh, and the fact that the same thing could happen to some other woman, I get upset. I'm getting ahead of myself and you've got every right to be offended. I shouldn't have come on so strong."

"Well, that's one thing we can agree on," she said, her anger dissipating some.

He shrugged. "Maybe we can start over and I'll try to be less offensive."

She couldn't help smiling. "Frankly, I'm not interested in making this enjoyable. What I'd like is to get it over with."

He nodded. But she couldn't help noticing the way he was staring at her—it wasn't the look of curiosity endured by the disabled.

"What?" she prompted, growing uncomfortable under his scrutiny. "Why are you looking at me that way?"

"Pardon me for sayin' so, Jane, but I was noticing you're a damned fine-looking woman. My sister, Leigh, was a beauty, too. J.T. has taste. I give him that."

She wasn't sure whether to be flattered or outraged. "I'm sure Jeremy'd be thrilled you find a redeeming feature in him."

His expression hardened. "Believe me, I wasn't tryin' for a compliment for old J.T."

"No, I suppose not."

Brady checked her out again in a casual, almost-brazen way. Jane shifted uncomfortably as his eyes roamed over her.

"So tell me, will you be getting out of that wheel-chair or are your injuries permanent?" he asked.

"My doctor is optimistic I'll recover, but there's some uncertainty. It'll be a while before we know how fully."

He rubbed his jaw. "Tell me, you didn't meet J.T. un-til after you were injured, isn't that right?"

"Yes, why?"

"Lord knows, it fits with the pattern."

"What pattern?"

"J.T. has a nose for vulnerable women. Leigh was desperate to be in love when they met. He knew ex-actly what she needed and gave it to her. The second wife was neurotic."

Jane bristled again. "Jeremy's kind and understand-ing, Mr. Coleman—"

"Brady."

"Brady. It's you who's seeing evil in him—and with-out cause, in my opinion. Maybe you've got the prob-lem. Has that occurred to you?"

"I've got a problem, ma'am. You're right about that. I feel a hatred and a loathing I can't get rid of. I never did cotton to J.T., but after Leigh's death I hated him. I'll be the first to admit it."

"And I suppose it's never occurred to you that you could be wrong about Jeremy."

"I know I'm right, Jane."

She swallowed hard. Brady had a steely certainty that was unnerving. And there was passion in him that was frightening in its intensity. If she wasn't dealing with a psychopath, she was certainly dealing with a man possessed.

"Maybe it's time we get to specifics," she said. "If you have a case to make, then maybe I ought to hear it."

"My briefcase is in the car," he said. "Mind if I grab it? I have three years of files on J.T. and I want to be accurate."

Jane sighed wearily. "No, go ahead."

Giving her a wink, he headed for the entry. Jane watched him go, wondering if he was a crackpot with an agenda of his own. But how could she not listen to him? Brady seemed convinced her life was at stake, and was even offering to prove it.

Jane looked down at her ring, feeling a surge of uncertainty. Only two nights earlier Jeremy Trent had slept in her bed. Now a cowboy from Texas with sincere blue eyes and a lazy grin was claiming Jeremy was a con artist, or worse. None of it made sense, not even the diamond ring.

Brady returned then, ambling across her great room as if he owned the place, leather briefcase in hand. He was simple on the surface, complex underneath. Just how wily he was, she wasn't sure.

"Lord, this is beautiful country," he said with good humor. "Your people own much of it?"

"My grandfather owned quite a bit of land on the peninsula at one time," she replied, "but most of it was sold years ago. The family still has some commercial property, and this place is mine."

"I'd hate to guess what prime land sitting on the ocean like this goes for," he said. "I'm sure it's mind-boggling compared to Texas rangeland that won't bring in more than a few hundred an acre." He settled back into the chair, his briefcase resting on his knees.

"Apples and oranges," she said, staring at the briefcase.

"Don't I know it. I've got a couple thousand acres off Nueces Canyon, myself. That's up in Edwards County. Sure you've never heard of it. Hundred miles northwest of San Antonio. Rocksprings, the county seat, doesn't have but twelve hundred people."

"Sounds charming."

"Not half so charming as your sarcasm, Doctor. But I can't blame you," he said, looking around. "I'm sure folks in Pebble Beach believe they died and went to heaven."

"I'm sorry. I didn't mean to sound snide."

"Don't apologize. There aren't many folks as chauvinistic as Texans." He grinned. "That's chauvinism in the original sense of belligerent jingoism, not sexism."

"Yes, I know," she said, "named after the French general in World War I."

"I believe Nicolas Chauvin was a soldier in the Napoleonic era, Jane," he replied mildly. Then he added with a wink, "But what's a hundred years among friends?"

She gave him a tight smile. "Apparently you don't just ride horses and brand cows."

"I don't run any cattle, as a matter of fact. I just look like I do."

"What's your profession?"

"I'm in oil. Thought I mentioned that."

"Perhaps you did."

"I'm a wildcatter, to be precise. A prospector of sorts. Most of my leases are down in Zavala County. You might have heard of the Austin Chalk."

"No, I'm afraid I haven't."

"They're pulling hundreds of millions of barrels out of those fields."

"That must be lucrative."

He smiled. "For the people with the right leases, it is. I'm not among them, unfortunately. But like most fellas in the business, I'm ever hopeful."

"Sounds like a fascinating profession."

"Oh, I've had my thrills. Not long after I got into the business we hit a gusher. That baby was putting out four hundred barrels an hour and we thought we were in hog heaven until it stopped after a few days. We hit a little pocket of oil with a lot of pressure. Up close, the ol' girl had hair on her lip."

"Charming way to put it."

He grinned. "Sorry... You live among good ol' boys . . . you talk like 'em after a while. The well didn't produce what she promised is what I mean to say. My cornucopia ended up costing me damn near a million bucks." He shrugged. "Chasing oil is like chasing the fountain of youth, though. Keeps you young."

"I thought it was chasing women that kept a man young."

Brady chuckled. "You said it, Jane. I wasn't about to." He winked and opened the briefcase.

She watched him perusing through the files, her heart picking up its beat.

"So, what kind of medicine do you practice?" he asked.

"Pediatrics."

"How is it you don't have a couple of rug rats of your own? Do the fellas out here lack confidence, or are you the discouraging type?"

She could tell he was playing with her, but she refused to acknowledge it. "I suspect it has more to do with me than the men I've met. I'm not the type to collect marriage proposals. There are better measures of self-worth."

Brady put the briefcase on the floor and held up a paper he'd taken from his files. He glanced at it, his expression sober. *"The State* versus *Jeremy Wells Trent,"* he said, as though reading. "I guess this is what we're here for, isn't it?"

"Is it the *State* versus *Jeremy,* or *Brady* versus *Jeremy?"*

He gave her a hard look. "You're right. I'm not objective when it comes to my sister. But the evidence is enough to make any fair-minded person wonder."

"What *is* your evidence?"

Brady looked down at the paper, his expression grim. "Fact. Leigh and J.T. were having marital problems. Two days before she was murdered she called me, all upset because Jeremy was doing something weird. Wouldn't tell me what. I thought he might've been abusing her, but she wouldn't say. But she did want me to convince him to see a shrink. She felt he needed help. That's no smoking gun, but it sets the stage."

"So far, I haven't heard anything remotely incriminating."

"I'm just getting started, darlin'. Fact. My sister was murdered in her bed. Strangled somewhere around nine in the evening. There were signs of a struggle. Violent struggle."

Jane felt her stomach tighten.

"Here's the clincher. "The police lab technicians found bits of J.T.'s skin under Leigh's nails. The middle and third finger of the right hand, the small and third finger of the left. There were scratches on J.T.'s body consistent with a struggle. The police have photographs of his back."

She suddenly felt sick. "Is that true?"

"Yes, it's all documented."

"Then why didn't they arrest him for the murder?"

"Because ol' J.T. fixed himself up a very clever alibi. And the story has enough of a ring of truth to it that the prosecutor didn't think he could make a case, not one that would hold up to the standard of proof—'beyond a reasonable doubt.'"

"What did Jeremy say?"

"He claimed he and Leigh were sleeping after having had sex—rough sex. He says he was awakened by an intruder. J.T. and the guy struggled, and the guy knocked J.T. out. J.T. swears he woke up later—he doesn't know how much later—and found the intruder choking Leigh. J.T. got his gun, shot and killed the guy. When he checked Leigh he found she was dead. At that point he called the police."

Jane swallowed hard. "Why couldn't that be true?"

"If it is, that would mean the guy—who turned out to be a petty street criminal by the name of Spike Adamson—had killed Leigh while Jeremy was unconscious."

"So?"

"Granted, the police confirmed that Adamson had come in the window—his footprints were in the flower bed outside—and that he died in Leigh's bedroom of a gunshot, as J.T. claimed. But none of the intruder's flesh was found under Leigh's nails. Only J.T.'s."

"Well, Jeremy said he and your sister had been having . . . rough sex. People do that, don't they?"

Brady smirked. "I won't inquire as to what happens in your bed, ma'am, but I know my sister, and *I* don't buy the rough-sex story for a minute. Not unless by rough sex he meant rape."

Jane shook her head. "You are not describing the man I know. Jeremy is a kind and affectionate person. He is *not* a pathological killer!"

"Jane, the rough-sex alibi is *his* concoction, not mine. You can check with the San Antonio police."

She shivered, knowing something was wrong. Brady had to be making this up, twisting the truth. To believe this she'd have to believe Jeremy was schizophrenic, and she didn't buy it for a moment.

"There's another fact that's damning," he continued. "The coroner placed the time of Leigh's death as much as two hours before Spike Adamson was shot. Admittedly it could have been as little as half an hour before the shooting. But even if it was only thirty minutes, that's a long time for Adamson to have been clinging to my sister's neck with J.T. layin' there unconscious. Don't you agree?"

"What did the prosecutor say about that?" she asked, the disbelief in her tone evident.

"That was the main reason he doubted J.T.'s story. But he still had to convince a jury that Adamson's breaking and entering was a coincidence—that J.T. lucked out and was given a perfect alibi. The prosecutor told me that mysterious intruders are the usual explanation given by defendants in spousal murder cases, but J.T. had the dead body to prove there'd really been one."

Jane laughed nervously. "Well, there you are! The intruder can't be explained away. Jeremy's story is perfectly reasonable. Your problem, Brady, is that you *want* to believe Jeremy's guilty. I can see that much, and I don't even know you!"

"How do you explain the time-of-death report?"

"Maybe there was a mistake. The prosecutors evidently didn't find it incriminating."

"Their problem was the burden of proof, not what they believed. As a matter of fact, they had serious doubts about J.T.'s story. But they needed more than the inconsistency in timing of death to charge him."

"Not to mention the fact that the man who really did it was lying dead on the floor!"

"Yeah, a man who my sister, struggling for her life, didn't manage to put a single mark on. Not one little scratch! Do you really buy that?"

Jane was starting to get as angry as he. "Nobody charged Jeremy with anything, did they?"

"Would you marry the man, knowing what you've heard?"

"You just want to believe Jeremy's guilty!" she retorted, her tone matching his. "This isn't about *me*, it's about *you!*"

Brady sat stony-faced, glaring at her. There was hatred in his eyes. For the first time, Jane actually felt frightened. He was breathing through his nostrils, trying to get control of his anger, she could tell. Now she was sorry she'd let him in, that she'd put herself through this.

Brady rubbed his jaw. "I think the bastard killed my sister," he said in a low, calm voice. "I think he hired Spike Adamson to break in on some pretext, God knows what. Insurance fraud, a practical joke, sexual perversion, who knows?"

"That's pure speculation."

"I know," he said. "If I could prove that's what happened, J.T. would have been on death row the last three years."

Her face turned ashen.

"Not a pretty picture, I know," Brady said. "What woman wants to wear the ring of a man who has *two* ex-wives having come to mysterious ends? Stranglings, drug overdoses, comas—it all jars with that charming Yankee blue-blood manner of his."

Jane took a deep breath to calm herself. "I respect your feelings about your sister . . . and about Jeremy, as well. But do you realize that you're asking *me* to find him guilty when the authorities wouldn't even bring charges? Who's being rational here and who isn't?"

"That's exactly what I'm asking you," he snapped.

She sighed with frustration. "If Jeremy killed your sister, what was his motive? Are you saying he was crazy?"

"No, it was good old-fashioned greed. I'm not sayin' the man doesn't have a loose screw, but he's a money-grubber. My sister was a very wealthy woman. Her father left her a fortune and ol' J.T. walked away with a good part of it. I asked Leigh once how long she thought Jeremy would stick around if she gave everything to charity. She didn't say anything, but we both knew the answer, much as she didn't want to admit it."

"Even if Jeremy did profit from your sister's death, that doesn't prove he killed her. He had money of his own. He came from a good family. He went to good schools."

"Do you know that, or is it somethin' he told you?"

"Jeremy is not one to brag, but good breeding is obvious."

"Oh, J.T. is a world-class actor, all right. But a good performance and reality are not the same."

"I suppose you're going to tell me he's a total fraud. That he doesn't have family money, that he bought his diplomas instead of earned them."

"Far be if from me to criticize a man because of who his parents were, sugar. I don't claim to be in the social register, myself. I have a great-uncle that was strung up by a lynch mob out in Pecos, and there's more than one card cheat in my family. But to my way of thinkin', there's a fundamental difference between bein' who you are and pretendin' to be something you aren't."

"You obviously have some dirt on Jeremy's family background you intend to share."

"Nothin' you wouldn't find if you took the time to look into it. Most of what J.T.'s got was weaseled out of his wives. He doesn't come from money. It's all pretense and lies."

"Money and virtue aren't the same, Brady."

"The honest poor, like me, don't have to lie."

"You assume Jeremy told me a tall tale about wealth," she said. "But he didn't. I made some assumptions."

"If so, he let you."

Jane shook her head. "Look, we could bicker all day. We're looking at the same man and seeing two different people."

"Forgive me, Jane, but that's your pride speaking."

"No less than your hatred speaks for you."

Brady chuckled. "You're quick. I'm surprised he took you in so easy. If you were half as suspicious of him as you are of me, you'd have shown him the door long before now."

She glanced at her watch. "Speaking of showing people to the door, you've had double the time I said I'd give you."

Brady grinned. "Even a Texan knows when they've outworn their welcome. I won't make you ask twice." He starting packing his briefcase.

She'd been tussling with him for half an hour. He'd made her angry, she'd even concluded he was half-nuts; but seeing that Brady Coleman was about to go, she was beginning regret it. Why, she wasn't even sure.

He closed the briefcase and fetched his coat. The anger and intensity were gone, the amiable smile had returned.

"I can't expect you to throw that ring in J.T.'s face on my word," he said, "but I'd hope you'd ask a few questions. The odds are good his third wife will meet the same fate as the first two. That's only my opinion, of course, but it's an informed opinion."

"I'll assume your motives in coming here were good," she said. "But I'll reach my own conclusions."

He chuckled. "In other words, thanks, but mind your own goldarn business."

"Californians aren't quite so blunt."

Brady Coleman slipped on his coat. "Texans are, ma'am. But I don't guess I have to tell you that after this visit, do I?"

Jane shook her head.

"Well, in case you're of a mind to think I made this whole thing up, let me give you this," he said, reaching into his shirt pocket. He removed a business card and handed it over. "Bobby Dalton is the assistant district attorney in Bexar County. He can confirm everything I've said. Call and ask him yourself."

Jane's heart tripped. He'd saved his highest trump for last! She studied the card, her heart sinking. "I'll think about what you've told me. I'll talk to Jeremy, too."

There was a touch of sadism in his grin. "I sure would like to be a fly on your wall."

"Don't be too sure of the consequences. I expect Jeremy to have a satisfactory answer for every accusation you've made." She gave him a steady look. "I don't wear this ring lightly."

"For your sake, Jane, I hope you won't be wearing it long." He picked up his briefcase. "I wouldn't want you ending up like Leigh or that woman in Connecticut. I couldn't live with myself unless I did everything I could to prevent it."

Jane said nothing. He started for the door, then stopped. "Oh, by the way, were you aware that J.T.'s Connecticut wife, Victoria, had been choked as well?"

"Choked? She overdosed."

"That's right. She had excessive drugs and alcohol in her blood. But there were also signs of trauma to her throat. The forensic medical people couldn't attribute her brain damage to that, but neither could they eliminate the possibility."

"Jeremy said nothing about that."

"I don't imagine he would. But it's in the police files."

"How did *you* get the information?"

"Nuckhols, a detective I hired, talked to a lab technician. He couldn't get photocopies of the report, but my money bought a verbal rundown on what's in the file."

"The police must have questioned Jeremy."

Brady nodded. "He gave them the same explanation as the first time. Rough sex." He looked back and forth between her eyes. "Interesting coincidence, isn't it? Somehow his partners end up dead or in a coma or something."

She shivered again, closing her eyes. "I don't think I'm up to discussing this further."

"Sorry. This hasn't been easy, I know." His expression was genuinely sympathetic. "Oh, let me give you one of my cards," he said, pulling a worn and bulging wallet from his hip pocket. He produced a dog-eared business card. "I need to get more printed up," he said, apologizing as he handed it over.

Jane looked at the card. It had his name, with the title, "President," under it. In the lower corner it said, "Coleman Oil," with a San Antonio address and phone number.

"I'm also the janitor," Brady said, "but I didn't see any point of putting that on the card, too."

"My grandfather started modestly," she replied.

"You want to see modest, Jane, I'll show you modest."

He dug through the wallet again, producing a frayed photo of a young Brady Coleman in jeans, boots and a cowboy hat, standing in front of a trailer. He was holding a hand-lettered sign that read The Buck Starts Here.

"That was me standing in front of my office just after I started my company," he said. "That's the good news. The bad news is it's still the same office pretty near a decade later, and its even shabbier than it was then."

"At least you're still in business."

"Shh," he said, holding his finger to his lips. "Wouldn't want my creditors to hear."

She laughed. The anger and intensity were gone. He was a different man now—the congenial, good-natured cowboy who'd come to her door.

"You seem well enough adjusted."

"I learned to be stoic. Like the man said, 'O money, money, money, I'm not necessarily one of those who think thee holy,/ But I often stop to wonder how thou canst go out so fast when thou comest in so slowly.'" He chuckled. "Ogden Nash."

"You *are* a reader, aren't you?"

"When you live in the hills you either hunt, breed, get a satellite dish, or you read. I read."

"You're full of surprises, Brady."

"I've run on more than is justified," he said. "Sorry to come in here and dump on you the way I have."

"Don't worry about it," she said.

"Will you be all right?"

She smiled appreciatively. "Of course."

"I'm kind of uncomfortable, leavin' you here alone."

She shook her head. "No, really. I'm fine."

"Can I look in on you tomorrow?"

The question surprised her. "Well...I don't...know if ..."

"I'd feel better knowing you're all right. Maybe you'd indulge me if I promised to stick to lighter subjects."

His smile seemed so open and friendly and warm, she found herself wanting to say yes. But when she reminded herself why he'd come and what he'd done, she knew she had to put him off.

"Why don't you call me in the morning and we'll discuss it?"

"All right. Around ten a good time?"

"Yes, that's fine."

Brady Coleman offered his hand. She reluctantly took it. "You've got a damned sweet smile," he said. "I wish I could have brought you joy instead of sorrow."

"You've got no obligation to me."

"I feel I do. Men can be sentimental, you know," he said.

He hadn't let go of her hand. She looked down at it, then into his incredible blue eyes. There was no question he had a powerful effect on her—one that was difficult to describe.

Brady gave her hand a final squeeze and headed off for the entry. "Come turn this dead bolt, you hear?" he called over his shoulder.

"I will," she replied in a weak voice, although it was probably too faint for him to hear.

Jane heard the door open, then close. She sat in silence, practically in shock. She looked down at the diamond Jeremy had given her, seeing it with different eyes. Two former wives—one murdered, the other in a coma. How, in the course of not much more than half an hour, could her world have been turned on its head? Wasn't it enough that she'd been laid up for six months and very nearly paralyzed for life? How did she deserve this on top of everything else?

5

"I'M SORRY, MA'AM," the girl said with a soft drawl, "but Mr. Dalton is in court. We don't expect him back until mornin'. Can I take a message?"

"Perhaps you can have him call me collect," Jane said. "I'm in California." She gave the girl her number and hung up, frustrated.

She'd hoped the phone call would help her get to the bottom of the matter. God knows, after her agonizing conversation with Brady, she didn't want any more uncertainty. She needed to find out once and for all whether he was a crackpot or if he was telling the truth. But the more she thought about Brady Coleman, the more certain she was that he wasn't crazy. Passionate, yes. Determined, definitely. But not nuts.

His thirst for revenge could have blinded him, however. Just because he believed what he was saying, didn't make it true. And anyway, she wasn't about to condemn a man she'd come to care for on the basis of unproved accusations—however sincere or well-intended they might be.

The truth would have to wait. She'd talk to the prosecutor tomorrow, and when Jeremy called this evening—as he was almost certain to do—she'd discuss the matter with him, too. Chances were he'd explain everything. But even as she thought that, Jane had doubts. The horror story Brady had related was no small thing.

There was no point in brooding, though. She put some music on and settled down to read. Opening the mystery she'd started days earlier, she realized it was a poor choice, considering her mood. She wasn't able to keep her mind on the story. Brady kept popping into her thoughts. She wondered about his sister and the sort of marriage she'd had with Jeremy. Rough sex, while not her taste, wasn't a crime. Not if it was consensual. But what did that say about Jeremy? Did he have a dark side that had escaped her? Or was the whole thing a lie?

Jane wished Manuela was there. She needed someone to talk to. Brady's accusations had given her the creeps. Damn him. Or would it turn out that she'd thank him?

The cordless phone rang, giving her a start. Her heart raced as she wondered what on earth could possibly happen next. But it was only Judy, one of her physical therapists, calling to ask if she could come by after lunch instead of the next day. Jane agreed.

She was pleased by the change in schedule. Judy's company would be welcome. Meanwhile she'd work at getting her mind off Brady's visit. She cleaned out her desk, she ate the lunch that Manuela had left for her in the refrigerator, but no matter what she did, Brady Coleman—both the man and his accusations—was in her thoughts.

She was glad when one o'clock came. She was just setting her plate on the counter next to the sink when the doorbell rang. Jane wheeled to the front door and let the therapist in.

"You must be doing well to spend the day alone," Judy, a slight, freckle-faced woman said as she took off her jacket and put it in the hall closet. "Wayne said you were doing better. He'll be back next week, by the way."

"I hope he enjoys his vacation."

"I'm sure he will." Judy moved behind her wheelchair. "Is your table still in the bedroom?"

"Yes."

She pushed Jane toward the bedroom wing. "I was looking at your file," she said. "Wayne's note said the next step would be building strength in your legs, regenerating muscle. He thought your flexibility was good."

"Yes, and I haven't had much pain for a couple of months."

"It sounds like you're ready to start putting some weight on your legs, then."

"Wayne has had me doing it when I get on and off the table."

"And you've gotten stronger?"

"Maybe a little."

"Good."

They entered the master suite. Judy set up the folding massage table. Jane wheeled over as the therapist prepared to help her up.

"This'll be a chance for you to use those legs," Judy said. "I'll do most of the lifting, but once your upper body is on the table, try supporting your legs. Dr. Krinski wanted you to begin challenging yourself."

When Judy moved in front of the wheelchair, Jane put her arms around the therapist's neck. "Let's lift together," Judy said. "Then we'll stand for several seconds. Ready?"

Jane nodded and together they lifted until Jane was upright. "My legs feel like rubber," she said. "I'm not supporting myself."

"You're carrying much more weight than you think."

"Maybe, but I'm not ready to go dancing, that's for sure."

Judy laughed. "Maybe not with me, but I bet with the right man you'd be inspired."

Oddly, the person who came to mind was Brady Coleman, not Jeremy. Why would she think of him?

Judy helped her lean against the table. That way her weight was somewhat supported but she had to use her legs to keep from slithering to the floor.

"That's good, Doctor. I bet in a month you'll stand without support."

"Think so?"

"Yep."

Her legs began to quiver so Judy swung her up on the table. "That's enough. Next week you can try the parallel bars."

"Yeah," Jane said sardonically. "I'll be dancing in no time."

"Have a special guy who's waiting to take you?"

Jane felt a knot forming in her chest. She couldn't speak.

"I'm sorry," Judy said. "I shouldn't have asked a personal question."

"That's all right," Jane managed. "I suddenly realized I don't know how to answer. Till this morning I'd have said yes."

Judy fell silent but Jane saw her glance at the diamond on her finger. On an impulse, Jane pulled the ring off. "Would you mind putting this over on my nightstand?" she asked.

Judy looked at the ring as she carried it over. "Sure is pretty."

"It's a friendship ring," Jane said, feeling she had to explain.

"You have some friend, I'll say that." Judy returned to the table, smiling down at her.

Jane felt a surge of anxiety. *Some friend*. The words rang in her ears. When all was said and done, would Jeremy still be her friend, or not?

THE REST OF THE afternoon was oddly tense. Jane felt restless and frustrated. No matter what she did, her mind was on her situation—especially her relationship with Jeremy. If he was a cold-blooded killer, as Brady claimed, why hadn't she seen it? Was she that needy and vulnerable, that easy to exploit? Or was Brady the exploiter, the con man?

Over the weeks she'd never given the question of Jeremy's motives much thought. She hadn't needed to, because he'd only just raised the subject of marriage. Now, she wondered if he was after her money. The problem was, her information was limited. She required the help of a professional.

A couple of years earlier she'd had occasion to deal with the attorney for the mother of one of her patients. The lawyer, a woman named Melissa Krum, was very sharp. Jane had decided at the time that if she had a legal problem that required sensitivity, she would consult her. This seemed as critical a problem as she'd ever have, so she telephoned Melissa's office.

"Dr. Stewart, how are you?" Melissa said. "I was sorry to hear about your accident. I hope your recovery is progressing well."

"It has been, but something has come up and I could use some advice. Coming to your office would be a bit difficult for me now, but I was hoping we could consult over the phone."

"Certainly, Doctor."

"It's Jane, please."

"Okay, Jane, what seems to be the problem?"

Jane recounted everything that had happened, from meeting Jeremy to Brady's visit. When she'd finished, Melissa sighed.

"Sounds like you're caught between two scrapping dogs."

"The analogy's not bad," Jane said. "What does a person do in a situation like this?"

"It shouldn't be hard to find out how itchy Jeremy's palms are," Melissa said. "When you talk to him, why not say you've given his proposal a lot of thought and wonder how he feels about a premarital agreement. His reaction should tell you where he's coming from on the money issue."

"Sounds like a good idea."

"And even if you decide Jeremy's all right and you want to marry him, a prenuptial agreement may not be a bad idea."

"Okay. What about Brady?"

"The cowboy's more of a problem. He's not asking for anything, unless his objective is to eliminate competition and romance you yourself."

"Somehow I don't think that's his angle."

"Then he's either a well-meaning hothead or a Good Samaritan." There was a silence on the line as Melissa evaluated the situation. "I recommend you have a background check done on Mr. Coleman. That's usually a good place to begin."

"I like that idea."

"You might want to check into Mr. Trent's background while you're at it. It'll mean two investigators and it won't be inexpensive."

"No reason to be penny-wise and pound-foolish," Jane said.

"And there's no point in risking your life if Mr. Coleman's accusations prove true. If you have a Dr. Jekyll and Mr. Hyde on your hands, it would be good to know about it."

Jane shivered. "Could you make the arrangements?"

"Yes, I can."

"Do I need to send you some money?"

"A retainer would be nice."

"How much?"

"A couple of thousand will do for starters."

"You know, Melissa, I wish you could help solve all my problems so easily," Jane said with a sigh, as she said goodbye.

JANE WAS SITTING at the kitchen table. She'd just finished eating the dinner she'd popped in the microwave when Manuela came in the back door.

"Doctor, you should have waited. I could have fixed you a nice meal. Something with lots of vegetables."

"Don't be silly, Manuela. Lord knows, there's little enough I do around here to make me feel useful." She wheeled away from the table and turned her chair to face the kitchen. "Have you eaten yet?"

"Yes, with my sister and her grandchildren. It is good to be with them, but after a day there, the quiet of this house is always welcome."

"I used to feel that way when I got home from the office," Jane said ruefully.

Manuela's face fell. "I should not have gone. It is not so good for there to be too much quiet in a house," Manuela said. "Not good at all."

"That wasn't the problem."

"Oh?"

But before she could explain, the phone rang. Jane took it from the hook on her chair. "Excuse me," she said, pushing the button. It was Jeremy.

She watched Manuela gather her dinner dishes and head for the sink at the far end of the room. Jane's heart was pounding. She'd been expecting Jeremy's call but now that it had come she wasn't sure how to act. "Glad you phoned," she said, trying to hide her nervousness. "How's your trip going?"

"Miserable," he said. "I miss you dreadfully, Jane. And I've worried night and day about having given you that ring."

"Having second thoughts?" she asked as casually as she could.

He laughed. "To the contrary, I've been concerned that I hadn't properly communicated my feelings first. I hope you've adjusted to the idea."

She took a deep breath before she answered. "Let's say I've been giving your proposal a lot of thought."

"Shall I feel encouraged, then?"

"Well, I'm a bit concerned that we've never really talked about the future," she said, gathering her courage to go on. "Maybe it would be a good idea if we did."

"I can't agree more."

"We're both well-off, so money shouldn't be a factor. I was wondering how you'd feel about our having a prenuptial agreement . . . to keep things separate."

There was a stunned silence—at least she assumed Jeremy was stunned. Jane had a terrible sinking feeling, sensing her worst fears were being confirmed.

"Well," he finally said, "if you feel strongly about it, I suppose there's no reason why we shouldn't have an agreement."

"My father felt that if I didn't have children, my share of the estate really ought to go to charity."

Another silence.

"I'm sure you have plans for your estate, as well," she prompted.

"Actually, I haven't given it a lot of thought. It wasn't an issue in my other marriages." His tone was a bit clipped.

"You didn't have prenuptial agreements?"

"No. They didn't press for an agreement, nor did I." He sighed. "Maybe I'm too much of a romantic."

"I think romance has a better chance to flourish if money is taken out of the equation," she said firmly.

"You may be right, Jane."

"You've told me about having to walk away from your second wife's estate in the interests of family peace, but I never heard what happened with your first wife. If you don't mind the question, did you inherit much from her?"

"Several hundred thousand dollars," he replied without hesitation. "Most of the Channing wealth was in their enormous land holdings. Arlo Channing, my wife's father, planned to leave my mother-in-law a life estate in the ranch. On her death, Leigh was to get it in remainder. Arlo wanted to keep it out of the hands of his stepson."

"Your wife's brother?"

"Half brother. His name's Brady Coleman. I didn't know Arlo, but I can certainly understand his hatred toward Brady."

"Why's that?"

Jeremy laughed. "He's a shiftless, irresponsible, womanizing cowboy who likes to think of himself as an oilman. My in-laws were eccentric. My wife was the only halfway normal one. And her major fault was that she fell under her brother's spell. Brady had the last laugh, though."

"What do you mean?"

"Leigh left her interest in the ranch to him."

"You mean when the mother dies Brady will get everything?"

"Yes."

"But your wife left you her cash."

"Most of it. I wasn't even aware of her plans, Jane. My love for her was all that mattered."

Jane pondered his remarks. Every word had been the politic thing to say. But she hadn't expected to hear that Brady Coleman was his sister's heir. He might be poor for the moment, but once his mother died, he'd be wealthy. If anything, he'd profited more from his sister's death than Jeremy!

"Her death must have been a terrible blow." She cleared her throat, then continued. "You know, Jeremy, you've never told me how she died."

There was a long pause. "She was killed by an intruder. It's not a happy story. I'd rather we speak of more pleasant things."

"I didn't mean to bring up a painful subject."

"You're such a dear," he said wistfully. "I'd like nothing better than to hold you in my arms right now."

"Me, too," she replied weakly.

"A few more days and I'll be home."

"I'm looking forward to it."

Jane said goodbye and hung up after that, not knowing what to think. Jeremy had gotten awfully quiet when she'd raised the issue of a prenuptial agreement, but it might have been because of the problems over money he'd had in the past. He'd seemed content enough in the end. Was it an act? Or was he innocent?

Brady had proved to be less than forthcoming. He'd put on a poor-boy act, when he was heir to a fortune. Maybe he resented the fact that Leigh had left her money to Jeremy, and Jeremy resented the fact that Brady would wind up with the ranch. Maybe Melissa Krum had the situation pegged right—maybe she *was* stuck between two scrapping dogs, each hating the other.

Manuela came over to her. "How would you like it if I put a fire in the fireplace, *señorita?* And I can fix you a nice cup of coffee to enjoy."

"That sounds like heaven."

The housekeeper beamed. "Señor Trent, he is all right?"

"Jeremy's fine, Manuela. It's me I'm not so sure about."

The woman frowned. "What's wrong?"

"I badly need that fire and cup of coffee."

"If that's all it is, *señorita*, I will soon make you happy."

Manuela headed off to the great room to build the fire and Jane sat musing. If only it were that easy, she thought. If only it were that easy.

6

JANE, WEARING A pink bikini, and Jeremy were sitting side by side on the edge of the sailboat, the wind blowing in their hair. "I love you, Jane," he said, just before he pushed her overboard.

She found herself bobbing in the waves, uncertain what had happened, though unafraid. The water was amazingly warm, almost like a bath. She shut her eyes, wanting to relax. Then suddenly she felt a pair of strong arms around her. It was Brady.

"Hey, little lady," he said, "you look like you could use some help."

He pulled her closer and she was aware that he was naked. And her bikini had magically disappeared. Jane looked around, but Jeremy was nowhere in sight. Neither was the sailboat.

For some reason she was certain that Brady was standing on the bottom. He was holding her. She felt safe. The water was lapping at her breasts and her nipples were exposed. The air felt cool on her wet skin, but she didn't mind.

Brady slipped his hand under her bottom then, to pull her closer. When she wrapped her legs around his waist, she could feel his skin touching hers between her thighs. She didn't say a word. She didn't want to break the mood.

With one arm still cradling her, he eased her away from him until she felt the water between her thighs once more. Then his free hand began massaging her. She looked into his eyes and saw drops of water glistening on his lashes. His eyes were a deeper blue than the ocean. When she leaned forward to kiss him, his lips tasted salty. His tongue slid into her mouth and she moaned, liking the intimacy.

They kissed like that for several minutes. Jane felt as if they would be like this forever, floating together in the water, slowly making love as if time—all the time in the world—was theirs for the taking.

She moaned a second time when he slipped a finger inside her and began massaging rhythmically. She felt herself moisten and she strained against him. Brady must have understood her need because he slowly withdrew his fingers and pressed the head of his sex against her opening. Jane held her breath and Brady slid into her. Soon he was thrusting in and out of her, slowly building the tension, making her want more, always more.

She awoke then, her heart racing and as breathless as in her dream. She was deeply embarrassed when she realized what had happened, and with whom she'd done it. The most surprising thing was that she was glad it wasn't Jeremy she'd made love with. The thought of it with him made her shiver, but so did the fact that in her dream she'd made love with a man she didn't know at all!

Jane rolled her head toward the window, enjoying the lingering pleasure of her sexual dream. She didn't often have them—not that she could recall, anyway. How her subconscious had come up with Brady Coleman, she didn't know, except perhaps because he was a handsome stranger.

Jane pushed the call button on the nightstand, alerting Manuela that she needed to get up. In a minute the housekeeper was at her door, bringing with her the smell of bacon and coffee.

"You ready to get up from the bed, Doctor?" Manuela asked. "It's a beautiful day."

"Yes, so I see."

"You want breakfast?"

"Maybe I'll bathe first."

Manuela drew the bath. It was a production to get her from the bed to the wheelchair, and then from the chair into the tub. For some reason, the whole operation bothered Jane more today than it usually did.

For months now she'd needed help to do the simplest tasks. And why? Because some stupid kid who had too much to drink had taken off in his pickup truck and driven down the highway, hell-bent for leather. As long as she lived she'd never forget those headlights coming at her from around the bend. She'd been on the Coast Highway, returning from a dinner meeting with the head of the hospital. With the steep cliff on one side of her and the ocean on the other, there was nowhere to go.

In the blink of an eye the truck had crashed into her: The boy had been killed instantly. It was all such a waste. Months of her life had been irretrievably lost. Thinking about it angered her.

How different things would have been if she hadn't had that damn accident! Jeremy might not have made such a big impression on her if she hadn't been frustrated and vulnerable. And for that matter, Brady might not have made such an impression on her that she would have a sexy dream about him! She'd have been far too busy living her own life and practicing medicine to worry about such things. And yet, that was exactly what consumed her now.

Jane soaped her arms and chest, trying to decide how she felt about Jeremy now. She realized she didn't know. She wasn't any clearer about her feelings than she'd been the day before. A bit of Jeremy's luster was gone, but if his transgressions proved to be minor, she wouldn't hold it against him. And as Melissa Krum might say, the jury was still out on that.

When she finished bathing, Manuela came to fish her out of the tub and together they got her into her rose-colored jogging suit. They were wheeling through the house when Jane's cordless phone rang. She answered it as Manuela pushed her along.

"Miss Stewart," a man's voice said, "this is Bobby Dalton, deputy prosecutor in Bexar County, Texas, returning your call."

"Oh, Mr. Dalton, thank you so much for calling. I have a problem I thought you might be able to help me with."

"If I can, ma'am."

They'd come to the breakfast room and Jane signaled for Manuela to go on to the kitchen. She turned her attention back to her caller. "I'm engaged to a man named Jeremy Trent. I think you know him," she said. "Recently I've learned that the tragic death of his wife in San Antonio involved some rather unpleasant complications. To be blunt, I've been told Jeremy was questioned by the police regarding the possibility of his involvement in his wife's murder."

"Who told you that, Miss Stewart?"

"Brady Coleman. In fact, I'm calling at his suggestion."

"I might have guessed," Dalton said, sounding more than a little exasperated.

"Is there a problem with that?" she asked.

"Brady's free to say what he pleases, I expect, but he can't speak for the San Antonio Police Department, or for this office. We have no comment to make on a case or investigation, whether in the past or ongoing."

"I realize you can't discuss details. Frankly, all I wish to know is whether there's substance to the accusations, whether I need be concerned about the sort of person Jeremy is."

"All due respect, ma'am, that's not for me to say. Mr. Trent wasn't charged with a crime in this jurisdiction. If he had been, it would be a matter of record."

"I understand that, Mr. Dalton. I'd just like to know if you *personally* doubted Jeremy's story. I must know if I have reason for concern."

"I appreciate what you're sayin', Miss Stewart. But comment would be unethical, and it could expose me to a lawsuit. I can't discuss the matter, even off the record."

Jane sighed with frustration. "All right. If we can't talk about Jeremy, can we talk about Brady? He wasn't investigated, was he?"

"No, ma'am."

"But you know him, don't you?"

"Yes, I do. For the better part of twenty years. Brady and I played ball together in high school."

"Tell me, then, is he trustworthy?"

Bobby Dalton hesitated. "You're aware that the deceased, Mrs. Trent, was Brady's sister."

"Yes . . ."

"Well, then you understand how his passions might run high."

"Yes, Mr. Dalton, I'm very well aware of that. But is he a crackpot? So full of anger that he can't think straight?"

Again the prosecutor fell silent. Jane waited.

"Let me put it this way, ma'am," Dalton said. "Brady's got an independent spirit. Some say he's full of the devil at times, but he's no crackpot. He's not crazy."

"Then there is basis for his accusations."

"Now I didn't say that, did I? I'm commentin' on Brady's character, that's all. In my way, I admire him. In Texas, if a man zealously pursues his sister's killer, he's to be admired. You won't find many who will fault him for that."

"But he could be misguided."

"You'll have to be the judge of that, ma'am."

"You aren't making this easy for me, are you, Mr. Dalton?"

"It's not my place to give my opinion about someone's character or culpability except in the course of my duties, Miss Stewart." He paused for a second. "I do regret not bein' able to assist you more. For that I apologize. May I suggest you discuss the matter with Mr. Trent?"

"I intend to, thank you."

"Would there be anything else, ma'am?"

"No, Mr. Dalton. I've taken a good deal of your time. I appreciate you calling."

Jane said goodbye and hung up. She hadn't learned a thing except, perhaps, that Brady wasn't a raving maniac. There was respect for Brady in Bobby Dalton's voice. It then occurred to her that Brady's trip to California was as much or more for his own benefit as for hers. He clearly took responsibility for what had happened to his sister, and probably felt a campaign against Jeremy was the best way to absolve himself.

She was disappointed that the prosecutor hadn't given any subtle hints as to his personal convictions. Even some small sign would have been welcome.

Manuela brought her breakfast. After Jane finished eating, she decided to go out into her garden. It was pleasant outside. A shawl around her shoulders was all she needed.

Her bonsai trees hadn't been pruned for a while, so she had Manuela bring her her shears and she began working on the plants. Her father had given her her first bonsai when she was twelve and she'd loved them ever since. Her collection was nothing like his, but she enjoyed them, and the breeze was invigorating.

Her phone rang and Jane answered it, wondering what now.

"This is Brady Coleman, Jane," he said. "Good morning."

She felt her spirits lift. He'd said he would call, but she hadn't been certain he was serious. "Hello, Brady."

"Hope you slept well."

It was an innocent comment, but Jane imagined secret knowledge—that he knew she'd dreamed of making love with him. Fortunately he wasn't there to see her face. No doubt, it was as pink as her jogging suit. "I slept very well, thank you."

"I was concerned, seeing as how I ruined your day yesterday."

"I survived."

"I'm pleased to hear it," he said. "Would it be all right if I looked in on you?"

"It's kind of you, Brady, but I don't see the point. I've heard what you had to say about Jeremy. Even if I don't accept your view of him in the end, you've alerted me to some things I needed to be clear about. I'm grateful for that."

"You're going to check J.T. out, then."

"Yes."

"Well, I feel better. If you start asking questions, you'll get to the bottom of it. And as long as you're open-minded, I'm not worried what you'll conclude," he said.

"Well, you've done your duty and can return home now." She cleared her throat. "Are you headed back to Texas right away?"

"No. We don't have to say goodbye just yet."

"Oh?"

"I know you don't want to talk about J.T. anymore. Frankly, I'd just as soon not talk about him myself. But there isn't any reason I can't drop by and pay my respects, is there?"

"It's nice of you to offer, but there's no need to come all the way out here."

"I'm already sittin' in your driveway, Jane. Won't be much trouble strollin' to your door."

She laughed. "Are you serious?"

"Yep. I know it's pushy, droppin' in uninvited, but to turn me down, you'd have to be as rude as I am."

"I'm understanding you better all the time, Mr. Coleman," she said with a chuckle.

"I'd like to think that's good."

"I'm in my garden, puttering while I have my coffee. You can join me, if you wish."

"I'd like that, ma'am."

She smiled with secret pleasure. "My housekeeper will let you in." She hung up the phone and called to Manuela, explaining she had a visitor out front. While she waited, Jane wondered if Brady had more surprises up his sleeve, or if this would be just a social call, as he claimed.

She looked down at herself, wishing she'd dressed differently. Maybe it was time to start making an effort again. Jane glanced toward the house, wondering what was taking Manuela and Brady so long. It was another minute before she saw them at the kitchen window. Manuela was getting a cup and saucer from the cupboard and Brady was chatting with her.

It wasn't until the door opened and they came onto the patio that Jane realized they were speaking Spanish. Manuela giggled at something he said, clearly charmed.

"Here is Señor Coleman, *señorita*," the housekeeper announced. "I already get him some coffee. Can I bring you some more?"

"No, thank you, Manuela."

The housekeeper nodded to Brady, who was holding a cup and saucer in his hand, "*Con permiso, señor*." She smiled at Jane and went back inside the house.

"You seem to have a way with the ladies," Jane said as he took her hand, half shaking it and half holding it.

"It pleased her that I spoke a little Mexican with her," he said. "I knew a few *caballeros* who hailed from the same neck of the woods as her people. We talked about that a little."

"So you're a linguist, too," she said, removing her hand.

"You spend enough time around the campfire with the *vaqueros* or tippin' tequila in the barroom, it comes to you, eventually."

Jane noticed he hadn't said, "Or romancing the *señoritas*," but she assumed that part. "Please sit down,

Brady," she said, gesturing toward the garden table and chairs.

She rolled her chair over, setting her shears on the table next to her empty coffee cup. Brady sat catty-corner from her, crossing his legs. He was dressed in jeans again, but he had on a different shirt. His handsome good looks and blue eyes were as imposing as before. He rested his saucer on his lap and sipped from the cup. He noticed her noticing his boots.

"Alligator's off the endangered list now," he said, then added with a wink, "not that they were when I got the boots."

"They're unique."

"Status symbol where I come from. In my case, a symbol of past glory." He chuckled. "Apart from my spread, the boots are all that's left of that false gusher I hit. Paid five thousand for them twelve years ago. They've been resoled twice, which sort of gives you an idea of how business has been."

"Your modesty is endearing, Brady, but now that I know the truth, it's ringing a bit false."

"Which truth is that, sugar?" he asked, sipping his coffee.

"The one that says you aren't the poor country bumpkin you make yourself out to be."

He frowned. "What do you mean by that?"

"Yesterday you gave me this poor-boy act, neglecting to mention that you're heir to a major fortune—the ranch your sister left you."

"Who you been talkin' to?"

"Jeremy told me the rest of the story."

"So, you discussed my visit with ol' J.T."

"Actually I didn't. We discussed his past when he called last night. I asked about the financial consequences to him of Leigh's death. In passing he told me that her interest in the family ranch went to you."

Brady looked at her unflinchingly. "So you came to the conclusion I'm a liar."

"No, but it's interesting you represented yourself one way, when the facts are different. It made me wonder about other things you've said."

"You know that I only have a remainder interest in the ranch and it's subject to my mother's life estate."

"Yes, you get it when your mother passes away." She watched his expression carefully, looking for a sign of guilt.

Brady grinned. "Well, I'm not expectin' that anytime soon. Mama's fifty-eight. Her daddy lived to be eighty-eight, her mama to ninety-three. I figure she's got another thirty-five or forty years, minimum. It's a little soon for me to start spending my great wealth." He gave her a level look. "Besides, with Leigh having been so much younger than me and female, I always assumed she'd outlive me by twenty years at least. And there was nothing to stop her from changing her will if she wanted. Are you suggesting I had something else to gain by my sister's murder?"

"I'm not suggesting anything, Brady. It's just that you're trying to tell me things about Jeremy I didn't know, and he's doing the same with you. If you want to know the truth, I think this whole thing is about you and him."

"It is."

"Then why drag me into it?"

"Because the nice guy in me doesn't want it bein' about him and your family down the line a year or two."

"You really think that if I married Jeremy he'd hurt me?"

Brady stared directly at her, but didn't answer.

"You really do, don't you?" she said.

"If you'd call Bobby Dalton, you wouldn't have to rely on my word."

"I've already talked with him. He said he couldn't discuss the case."

"*What?*" Brady demanded, putting the cup and saucer down on the table. "He told you that?"

"Yes, and he didn't seem too pleased that you had me calling him, either."

"Why, that low-down coward! Bobby knows I wouldn't have had you call him unless it was important."

"I don't think the importance of the matter had anything to do with it."

Jane saw that he hadn't heard her. He was too upset. His face had flushed and he was mumbling. "Damned lawyers don't have the common sense of a rat."

He pulled his cellular phone from his coat pocket and began pushing the buttons furiously. Oddly, she found his earnestness endearing.

"Hello," he said into the phone. "Give me the number of the Bexar County prosecutor's office, will you, please?" He listened, then punched more buttons. He listened, shaking his head. "Hi there, darlin'," he said after a moment, "this is Brady Coleman. Put Bobby Dalton on the line, will you please? Well, I'm sure he's in conference. So am I. As a matter of fact, I'm sittin' out here in California with egg on my face, thanks to him. Tell him if he doesn't get on the line right now, I'm comin' back to Texas to separate him from his scalp."

He put his hand on the mouthpiece and said, "Sorry, but I'm tryin' to communicate a sense of urgency."

Jane smiled. "So I gather."

He waited, drumming his fingers on the table.

"Bobby," he said into the phone, "what in the hell are you doin' tellin' this little lady you can't discuss Leigh's case? ...I don't care how difficult your position is. That SOB should be behind bars and you know it. What are the taxpayers puttin' gas in that Cadillac of yours for, if it isn't to prevent a crime? ...I don't care about the law! This isn't a damned courtroom!

"We're talkin' about an innocent young lady who wants the benefit of your knowledge. Her life could depend on what you say, so talk from the heart. This is off the record, you've got my word on it. I'm puttin' her on now, so tell her what you think about Leigh's murder."

Brady leaned over, handing Jane the phone. "That's Bobby Dalton."

Jane put the phone to her ear. "Hello again, Mr. Dalton," she said. "Sorry to impose, but Brady feels I need to have this conversation with you."

Bobby Dalton laughed. "Thank goodness you were sitting there," he said. "That way I only got an earful and not cut to pieces." He sighed. "I hope you understand that what I'm about to say is not the official position of the prosecutor's office. If you make it public I'll be forced to deny it."

Jane felt her blood go cold. She looked into Brady's blue eyes. "I understand," she said slowly.

"I can't tell you whether your fiancé murdered his wife or not, but there's evidence that makes me very uncomfortable with his alibi. As a minimum, I have to tell you there are unanswered questions."

Jane listened to an analysis of the case that corresponded almost exactly to Brady's. The timing of Leigh Channing's death and the fact that the only evidence of a struggle was tied to Jeremy, not the intruder, were the most damning points.

"The trouble was, we had a corpse in the bedroom. It would have been hard to explain that away in court, when all you have on the other side is the testimony of lab techs and contradictory physical evidence. It's a prosecutor's nightmare."

Jane's heart was pounding. "Do you think Jeremy murdered his wife?" Jane asked, her voice thin.

"I don't know, ma'am. I have trouble believin' his version. It doesn't ring true, but that's mostly a gut instinct. In court I've got to deal with provable fact."

"I understand."

"You haven't spoken with Mr. Trent about this, I assume."

"Not in detail."

"As I told you earlier, it'd be wise for you to do so. But I'd appreciate it if you didn't mention this conversation. I'm speakin' candidly as a favor to Brady."

"I understand your difficulty, Mr. Dalton. Don't worry."

She glanced again at Brady, who signaled he wanted to speak again with Bobby Dalton. She handed him the phone.

"Listen, partner, I owe you a big night on the town," Brady said. "Give me a jingle when Laura's in Houston visitin' her folks." He grinned, giving Jane a wink. "No, don't worry," he told his friend. "I'll perjure myself if necessary to save your butt. This call never occurred, I don't care what Jane says.... All right, I'll be talkin' to you. Thanks again, Bobby."

Brady put the phone back in his jacket pocket. He stared at her, but he wasn't gloating.

"So, you weren't lying or exaggerating or . . . hallucinating," she said.

There was consternation on his face. "There's qualification in your voice."

"Mr. Dalton admitted he's uncomfortable with Jeremy's story, but he's not prepared to pronounce him guilty." Jane took a deep breath. "I'm not, either. Certainly not until after I've talked to him."

"That's all I was hoping for, Jane," he said, apparently content. "I'd be happy to be here when you talk to him."

"No," she said quickly. "It's kind of you to offer, but it would only make things worse. I have a feeling Jeremy would not be at all pleased to see you."

He grinned. "You've got that right."

"I have no desire to see a duel," she said.

"Somehow I don't think J.T. would be interested. He prefers his victims helpless."

Jane studied him. "You really hate him, don't you?"

The door to the house opened and Manuela came out with a pot of coffee in her hand.

"Maybe it's best we change the subject," Brady said. "When I came here this morning I hadn't intended to talk about J.T."

"More coffee, *señores*?" Manuela offered, coming to the table.

"*Por favor, señora*," Brady replied.

Jane declined. Brady held up his cup.

"*Muchas gracias*," he said after she'd poured.

"*De nada, señor*." Manuela smoothed her hair and smiled. Then she glanced at Jane. "He speaks very good

Spanish and he knows the country I came from in Mexico."

"So I understand," Jane said.

"Just ask if you wish more coffee, *señores*," Manuela told them, going off.

Brady watched Manuela return to the house. "Your housekeeper is real nice," he said.

"The regard seems to be mutual."

"Everybody likes a little attention, Jane. I do, and you probably do, as well."

She pulled her shawl around her shoulders, feeling oddly uncomfortable. Brady sipped his coffee, observing her.

"It's a little chilly out here. You getting cold?" he asked.

"I've been out for a while. I'd like to go inside, I think. But finish your coffee."

"I can take it in," he said, getting to his feet. Brady looked down at her. "You know, since we talked yesterday I've been wondering whether you ever get out of the house. Are you cooped up here all day, day in and day out?"

"I don't get out much except to see my doctor. Why do you ask?"

"I had a hunch you didn't see many people."

Jane wondered what he was driving at. "Occasionally friends drop in, but I don't pressure anyone to come. Manuela and I get by just fine."

"And then I'm sure J.T. is always coming to see you."

"Jeremy has been very good about visiting. Is that what this conversation's about?"

"No, no," Brady said, waving off the notion. "As a matter of fact, I was thinking that shutting yourself in was probably the worst thing you could do for your spirits."

"You're an expert in psychology as well as oil, I see."

He laughed. "Better at psychology, actually." He scratched his head. "I haven't had much of a chance to see Monterey yet. I thought maybe you'd give me a guided tour. For your trouble, I'll take you to lunch."

"It doesn't sound as if you'd accept my wheelchair as an excuse why I couldn't," she said.

"No, that's kind of the point I'm tryin' to make."

"Isn't the real point that you're taking a contrary position to what Jeremy would do?"

"Oh, I'm sure for ol' J.T., the more incapacitated, the better. Personally, I like my women to put up a bit of a fight. What's the sport in romancin' a gal who's sitting around feeling sorry for herself?"

His words shook her. "Is that how you see me, Brady?"

"I expect you're a handful, Jane, whether you're sittin' in that chair or not. But you've spent so much time lettin' J.T. hold your hand that the fight's gone out of you."

"You know, in your way you're as manipulative as Jeremy."

"Maybe, but there's one big difference. I'm thinkin' of you. J.T. thinks of himself."

"You're really very clever."

"Does that mean you're going to come with me?"

Just what his angle was, she wasn't sure, but his challenge had sparked something in her. Maybe she was more lonely than she thought. Or maybe he was right; she had been feeling sorry for herself.

"All right," she said. "I'll give you a tour and have lunch with you, but don't think for a minute I don't think that you're the biggest con I've ever met in my life. And you know what?"

"What, darlin'?"

"I bet you've broken the hearts of half the girls in Texas."

Brady threw back his head and laughed. Then he moved behind her wheelchair and pushed her toward the door.

"I see you're not denying it," she said.

"Darlin', if you've made up your mind what kind of fella I am, what good's it goin' to do me to deny it?"

7

BRADY GAZED OUT the wide plate-glass window of the restaurant. The view of the gray-green waters of Monterey Bay was beautiful. For the last several minutes he'd been watching an otter lolling on its back, trying to open an abalone shell. The waiter had pointed it out after Jane left for the ladies' room.

He and Jane had shared a companionable few hours. She'd taken his comment about a tour seriously, showing him Carmel and the mission, although they didn't get out of the car. She said it would be too much trouble, considering her wheelchair. The shops were apparently the main appeal of the village. He'd thought it was all sort of quaint. It made him think of quiche and white wine and guys in golf shirts.

Jane had been polite but distant—like someone going through the motions for a distant cousin. Brady wasn't sure if that was because she was still upset about the things he'd told her about Jeremy, or if it was him. But he hadn't pressed her. Instead, he'd confined his familiarity to little jokes.

After Carmel they'd taken the portion of the Seventeen Mile Drive that went along the coast, following it past Cypress Point, Bird Rock, Point Joe and Moss Beach. The scenery was spectacular—windswept cypress trees on rocky outcroppings, waves crashing into the land and sending saltwater plumes into the air.

They'd left the drive, then, and followed Highway 68 down into Pacific Grove. Monterey itself was pleasant—neat, clean and wealthy. It reminded him of parts of San Antonio. While they were driving around town, Jane had pointed out her office.

"Want to stop in and say hello?" he'd asked.

Jane had shaken her head. "No. They're closed for lunch anyway."

When he'd asked how long it had been since she'd visited, she'd admitted she hadn't been there since her accident. Knowing it would only depress her, she'd stayed away.

"Maybe that's something you need to overcome," he'd said, unable to resist the temptation to prod a bit.

"Maybe you need to stop trying to be my big brother," she'd chided.

He'd grinned, glad to get an honest reaction out of her, even if it was a negative one. "We'll discuss it after we eat," he'd said.

They'd come to Cannery Row for lunch. She'd seemed sort of embarrassed when he parked the car and the time came for him to help her into her wheelchair. Jane insisted she didn't want him lifting her, which seemed pretty silly, given the circumstances. He'd started to argue until he saw how upset she was. He'd caved in then, and helped her scoot from the car seat into the chair instead.

"You know," he'd said as he locked the car door and they began strolling along the sidewalk, "I'd think bein' a doctor, you'd handle this wheelchair business better."

"What can I say, Brady? I'm used to being in charge— in charge of the situation, in charge of my life. These past six months I've felt helpless. This is not normal for me and I hate trying to pretend that it is."

He'd stopped right in the middle of the sidewalk, in front of a curio shop, and had gone around in front of her chair, arms folded across his chest. "Want me to take you home? Would you rather not be here, Jane?"

She'd looked up guiltily. "I'm being childish. I'm sorry. It won't happen again."

They'd gone on to the restaurant. And although there weren't any more complaints from her, she was clearly distracted—even when he'd say something funny and make her laugh. And when she lapsed into silence, looked down at her ring finger and got a far-off look in her eyes, it was apparent what was going through her mind. His unmasking of Jeremy Trent had been a blow to her.

Brady couldn't have been happier about that. He'd done just what he'd set out to do—he'd supplied Jane with the rope. All that remained was for J.T. to hang himself.

Oddly, now that his task was done, he had no desire to hurry back to Texas. He wasn't sure why, but he figured it had more to do with Jane than with him or Jeremy. He felt protective of her. True, she was in a wheelchair. She was also in J.T.'s clutches. But that was only part of it. She inspired different feelings in him than most women. She was like the kitten he'd secretly loved as a boy or, for that matter, like Leigh—the one above all others he'd felt the need to nurture and protect.

That seemed strange. Injured or not, Jane wasn't helpless. She was emotionally shaky, but she was also smart, independent and self-sufficient. Normally he didn't get along with that type.

Brady was a throwback, and he knew it. He'd always known he was bucking the tide of change, but he also knew there were enough traditional girls to go around, especially in Texas. He'd never worried much what folks were doing in San Francisco or New York. For that matter, he didn't worry much about what they were doing in Dallas and Fort Worth. So why a sudden fascination with a doctor from California? On paper, they couldn't have been more different.

"So, has the ocean captured our landlubber's imagination?" It was Jane. She'd silently wheeled up to the table. He started to get up, but Jane motioned for him to keep his seat.

"I'm already sitting, so what's the point?" she said, moving her chair up to her place.

"Outmoded chivalry," he said. "I guess you modern girls don't value it much."

"We modern *women* appreciate a gentleman, Brady, so you needn't feel defensive."

He grinned, looking at her pretty face. "I was in junior high when women started burning their bras. I suppose it made such an impression on me that I haven't yet recovered. I was sort of thinking about that just now."

"Really?" she teased.

"As a matter of fact, I was thinking about you and another lady I knew once, a while back. It's been several years ago now. I can't even recall her name. She was an investment manager in San Antonio. She went slumming with me to a country-and-western dance hall on our only date. When I took her home, she said, 'I hope you don't find me too intimidating because the last thing I want is to emasculate a man. But I've got to be myself.'"

"And what did you say?" Jane asked.

He laughed. "You don't want to know."

"Yes, I do."

Brady shrugged. "I looked her in the eye and I said, 'Susan—'or whatever her name was '—after tonight I may not get it up for another month.'"

Jane's eyes widened. "You didn't."

"Yep, I sure did."

"And what did she say?"

"She said, 'Well, in that case, I guess there's no point in inviting you in.'"

Jane began laughing, shaking her head. "Brady..."

He waited for her to recover, then went on. "And I said, 'Not unless you'd be content havin' a cup of coffee and a little conversation, sugar.'"

"No, you didn't," she said, wiping her eyes.

He nodded. "Sure did."

"So what happened?"

He stroked his chin. "You're not afraid to ask a man a personal question, are you, Doctor?"

"Evidently you changed her mind about her powers of intimidation."

He chuckled, looking her dead in the eye until she blushed. She didn't press the point.

The waiter came and took their orders and after he'd gone, Jane said, "So, why were you thinking of me in connection with your lady friend?"

"I don't know. Quiche and wine, chili and beer, Texas and California, I suppose."

"Brady, you aren't the country bumpkin you like to pretend. I picked up on that five minutes after you walked in my door."

"You callin' me a fraud, Dr. Stewart?"

"I wouldn't go that far, but you're tricky."

"More like defensive, I think."

"What are you defending against?" she asked.

He stroked his jaw again, not sure why they were having this conversation. He gave her a questioning look as if to inquire if she really wanted to pursue the matter.

"You don't have to answer," she said.

"I guess I'm tryin' to understand why I have this urge to take you in, like you were a stray cat or something."

"Maybe you're more kindhearted than you give yourself credit for."

He shook his head. "Take my word for it, this is unlike me."

He watched her and she watched him until she finally turned to look out the window. He examined her face. She had delicate features, a well-shaped nose, and the most beautiful gray eyes.

It occurred to him that he had a crush on her. He couldn't explain it, except as an attraction of opposites. There was also this feeling that she needed him, needed his protection. It was very strong.

He wasn't used to that. His attraction to women had always been straightforward. Conquest was the game and he had formidable tools—charm and animal magnetism. He used them as necessary and the romance always took care of itself.

"What was Leigh like?" Jane asked, turning to him.

"She was a sweet girl, pretty. Headstrong, but fragile. Like most everybody, she wanted to be loved. Too much, maybe."

"You obviously were very fond of her."

"My mama and I were close, but I didn't want her to run my life, even when I was real young. My constant pulling away put a wall between us, especially after she remarried. When Leigh came along, I don't know why I felt so possessive of her, but I did.

"I was hurt when she married J.T. It wasn't because I was jealous. To the contrary, I wanted her to be happy. What upset me was that I knew she was making a mistake and I couldn't make her listen to me. I was resentful, and that's what hardened my heart. And then later, when she really needed me, I failed her. That's the burden I'm carrying now."

"You can't blame yourself, no matter what you did."

"I only had one little sister, Jane. I'll never have another."

AFTER LUNCH THEY decided to skip the Aquarium. Brady was driving her back home. They were coming up on Franklin Street when she suddenly told him to turn right.

"This isn't the way back to the freeway, is it?" he asked.

"No, it's the way to my office."

Brady drove in silence, a faint smile touching the corner of his mouth. Jane glanced over at him, knowing exactly what he was thinking.

"Well, at least you're not gloating."

"I think it's a good idea that you drop by."

"I probably should have called to warn them I'm coming in," she lamented.

Brady handed her his cellular phone.

"You've got an answer for everything, don't you?"

"Just trying to be helpful."

Jane wondered why. This had nothing to do with Jeremy. As far as she could tell, it had nothing to do with anything. Was it his way of showing compassion for the poor "stray"?

Jane dialed her office and told Kelly, the receptionist, she was going to drop by. Kelly greeted the idea warmly. "Wish you were coming in to see patients, though," she added. "It's a zoo today. Dr. MacKenzie is at the hospital doing an emergency C-section, Dr. Mendez is home sick with the flu, and Dr. Bosche is going crazy."

"I'll try not to get in the way," Jane told her, then hung up, thinking an office visit wasn't such a good idea after all.

When she told Brady they were busy and she'd feel like a fifth wheel, he scoffed. "A little adrenaline is just what you need. Whenever I start feeling lethargic I go out to a drilling site and get a little mud on my boots. Does wonders for the spirits."

"Why are you taking such an interest in my psychological well-being?" she asked.

"I suppose because everybody else seems to be holding your hand when what you probably need is a kick in the butt."

"Nicely put, Brady."

"Pardon my French."

She directed him to turn again. "You aren't the only one who's nagged me."

"Don't tell me J.T. was urging you to get out and make like a real person."

"No, but my doctor's been after me to get out of the house."

"Well, who listens to a doctor?" he said, giving her a wink.

"You obviously don't."

He reached over and pinched her cheek. "I have a feeling I'm just beginning to see the real Jane Stewart."

She felt herself color. Brady was a tease, but underneath that good-natured, down-to-earth facade there was a decency, too. She liked the guy, liked him a lot.

"It's in the next block, isn't it?" he asked, slowing.

"Yes," she replied. "Maybe you should park if you get an opportunity. I'd suggest taking my reserved space, but I'm not sure it's still there."

"If you've been excommunicated, it's your own fault, sugar." Brady patted her knee.

Jane noticed he'd let his hand rest there an extra moment or two before finally taking it away. It occurred to her then that for all his paternalism, there was something else going on in the back of Brady Coleman's mind. She thought of her sexy dream and something stirred inside her.

He probably had this effect on her because she'd never met anyone with his kind of sexual magnetism before. What surprised her was that as time went on, it seemed to be getting more intense. She'd have thought that the better she got to know him, the less effect he'd have on her.

Her whole situation was odd, now that she thought about it. One day she gets a ring from a man she hadn't even considered as a potential husband, the next she's being seduced by a man she has about as much in common with as . . . well, quiche and chili.

Brady parked half a block up from the medical building. But instead of getting out, he leaned back and gave her an appraising look.

"Do you want to go in yourself, or do you want me to come with you?" he asked, casually resting his arm on the back of her seat.

She was surprised by the question. "I thought you were the one who was so interested in seeing my office."

He shrugged. "It was just my way of getting you fired up."

"Oh, really?"

"I know I've been kind of pushy, so I wanted to give you the chance to do it your way."

He touched her hair with the tips of his fingers. The gesture struck her as curiously intimate.

"Thanks for your thoughtfulness, but I can't even get out of the car without help. Not unless I wanted to crawl along the sidewalk."

"Oh, I'll get you into your chair. I assume the building is wheelchair accessible."

"Yes, but I don't mind you coming with me. I'm doing it to prove to you I can as much as for any other reason."

"I'm flattered."

"You should be."

Brady brushed the backs of his fingers across her cheek in an affectionate, even loving way. She saw something in his eyes, an intensity that unnerved her. And she felt an energy, the most powerful she'd felt with him yet.

He was evidently as aware of it as she because after they'd stared at each other for a minute, he leaned over and kissed her lightly on the lips, then on the corner of her mouth.

"I've never kissed a doctor before," he murmured. "Thought I'd see what it was like."

"I've never been kissed by a cowboy before, so I guess we're even.

"No offense intended," he said.

"None taken."

A self-satisfied grin crept across his face as he opened the car door and got out. Jane drew a long breath to calm herself. First Jeremy, now Brady. It wasn't like her to be taken in by a man so easily. Maybe visiting the office was a good idea. Maybe what she needed was to get back to being her old self.

As Brady got her wheelchair out of the trunk, she looked at herself in the rearview mirror. There was a healthy glow on her cheeks and a sparkle in her eyes that had been missing for some time. Being kissed by a cowboy was pretty damned good medicine, it seemed.

8

DARKNESS WAS FALLING as they arrived back at her place. Brady turned off the engine and Jane lay against the headrest, staring out at the rose-and-gold sky.

"What a day," she said. "I'm exhausted."

He took her hand. "I hope I didn't push you too hard."

"It wasn't you. It was playing doctor again after such a long sabbatical."

"Is that what 'playing doctor' means out here? In Texas, it means something a little more provocative."

Jane gave him a poke with her elbow. "You were right that visiting the office would get my adrenaline flowing. I'm tired, but I feel exhilarated at the same time."

"I didn't expect you to jump back into the saddle when I suggested we drop by."

She shook her head. "I didn't, either. But when the little Jiminez girl came in feverish and Joan was already up to her ears in sick babies, I couldn't just sit there."

She squeezed the teddy bear in her arms. While she'd been treating patients, Brady had gone downtown to the toy store and had picked up a dozen stuffed animals for the crying children in the waiting room. He'd saved a golden brown bear with a big red bow for her, saying she was a patient, too. She'd hugged it all the way home, recalling the secure feeling her childhood teddy bear had given her during difficult moments.

She'd told him getting the stuffed animals was a sweet gesture and she'd appreciated his patience and understanding. More than one mother had commented on the "nice man" in the waiting room.

"It was a change of pace," he'd said. "Besides, everybody wants to feel useful. What else is a funny-sounding Texan in alligator boots going to do in a place like Monterey?"

By the time they'd left the office Jane was seeing Brady through different eyes. When she'd asked if he was always that way, he'd admitted he wasn't. Other than having occasionally dated a single mother, he hadn't been around kids much.

Brady reached over and gave her chin a tweak. "You look real natural with that bear in your arms, Doctor. You aren't secretly clinging to your childhood, are you?"

"Everybody does in one way or another."

"There's a lilt in your voice I haven't heard before," he said. "And it sounds pretty damned good, if I do say so."

"This must sound contradictory, but I feel more like myself than any time since the accident. And it's all thanks to you."

"Well, I'm glad."

"How is it you never wanted to be a father, have children?"

Brady looked over at her in the falling light. The shadows had muted his features, but she could tell by his expression he'd taken the question seriously.

"Maybe I'm old-fashioned, but I always thought a man ought to think in terms of a wife first and children later."

"I guess that was really my question. Is it chance that there hasn't been a woman you loved enough to marry, or are you a bachelor by design?"

"I've always been a free spirit, Jane."

"Meaning free of commitment and entanglements?"

"Yes, I suppose so. Never really hungered for a different life. My old man was the same way."

"So it's genetic."

"You don't like that excuse."

She smiled. "Doctors like to think every condition is treatable."

"No, that's not what you really mean. Guys like me are unsettling to the female sense of order. That's what you're reacting to."

"Sounds to me like you've had this conversation before."

"I like to think of my bachelorhood as a kind of public service," he said, ignoring her comment. "Why pass on the defective Coleman gene to torment the next generation of women?"

"You're selling yourself short, Brady. You've got a lot to give. I've seen it in the brief time I've known you."

He tweaked the nose of the bear. "Coming to see you was my good deed for the year. Now I won't feel so bad going back to my life."

"Is that really the way you look at it?"

"More or less."

She looked over at him, feeling a strange sadness, but also a yearning. She wanted something more—more of him, more of what they'd shared during this remarkable day.

"And now that you've done your good deed, are you heading back to Texas?"

"That's the plan."

"When are you leaving?"

"I wanted to stay long enough to satisfy myself that your eyes are open about J.T."

"My eyes are open. And I'm in a questioning mode. That's all I can promise you."

"I guess I can't expect more than that, Jane."

"No, you've done all you can."

He stared out at the muted grays of the evening and Jane did, as well. She sensed his frustration and understood it. She had the same feeling of misconnection. Quiche and chili. Surf and chaparral. California and Texas. *Ciao* and *adiós*. Some things were so obvious they didn't need saying.

"I've got a flight booked out of Frisco for the day after tomorrow," he said, sounding almost sad.

"What are you going to do tomorrow?"

"I didn't have anything planned. I suppose I ought to take advantage of being here, though. I've already had the two-bit tour of Monterey. What else is in the neighborhood?"

"Well, you should drive down to Big Sur. It's just twenty miles down the coast. Some people say it's the most spectacular stretch of coastline anywhere."

"Guess I shouldn't miss it, then."

"No, you'll be glad." Jane hugged her bear.

Brady looked at her, the expression in his eyes only just discernible in the near darkness. "Well, it's been an eventful day and I know you're tired."

"Absolutely exhausted. I might skip dinner and go right to bed."

"Maybe you'll swallow your pride and let me carry you into the house, rather than struggle with the wheelchair."

"I'm already clutching a teddy bear, so why not go all the way?"

He smiled so broadly the white of his teeth almost glowed.

"What's so funny?"

"Going all the way must mean something different here than it does back home, too."

Jane shook her head. "Nope. It means the same thing to perverts here that it means in Texas. Your bachelor mentality is as obvious as those boots of yours, Mr. Coleman."

"You gotta admit I can be amusing."

"Just barely."

He laughed and got out of the car. "I'll alert Manuela that we're home."

He sauntered up to the front door and rang the bell. Manuela answered and, after Brady explained the plan, she peered out into darkness at Jane, waving.

Brady returned to the car and opened the passenger door. "Ready?"

Jane put her arms around his neck, her bear still in her hands. He lifted her effortlessly. During her convalescence she'd lost weight, but Brady's strength was evident. He seemed to enjoy holding her and Jane liked it herself. She cradled her teddy bear against her breast as they went to the house.

"*Hola, señorita!*" Manuela greeted. "Did you have a big day?"

"Brady took me to the office and I treated patients," Jane said cheerfully as they stepped through the door.

"Good for you!" the housekeeper said, beaming.

Jane indicated the way and Brady carried her through the house. As they went, he inhaled her scent.

"Anybody ever tell you that you smell like a Texas rose?"

"No, and it's unlikely that anybody would. I've never been to Texas."

Brady stopped dead in his tracks. "What?"

She shook her head. "Never have."

"Well, soon as you're on your feet you'll have to come to San Antonio for a visit."

He was saying it to be polite, but she wanted to think that he halfway meant it. "Will you give me the two-bit tour, if I do?"

"Sure. I'll show you the Alamo and every respectable dance hall in town," he said, continuing on back to her bedroom. "And there are a million great Mexican restaurants, and even a few fancy froufrou places that serve snails and things like that."

"Bet you like French cuisine more than you're willing to admit, Brady Coleman."

He shook his head. "You're not as easy to deceive as I thought. This trip probably wasn't even necessary."

He laughed as if he were teasing, although she wasn't at all sure if he meant it. In truth, there was no telling how things with Jeremy might have gone. She wanted to think the issues Brady raised would have come up anyway, but she couldn't be certain that was true.

"Well, I feel better for having come," he said.

Jane nodded. "I'm glad you did."

They entered the bedroom and Brady put her down on the bed. Manuela, who'd followed them through the house, came up beside him.

"You want some dinner soon, Doctor?" She glanced at Brady, and Jane took that to indicate she was prepared to fix something for them both.

"I'm so pooped, Manuela, that I'm going to take a nap before anything else. I'd forgotten how exhausting kids can be."

"You want nothing at all?"

"How about if you fix me a bowl of soup? I'll have it here, if you don't mind."

"Of course not, *señorita*. I will fix it now." She left the room.

Brady, his hands on his hips, peered down at her.

"I feel like such a wimp," she said. "But I know now I can do it."

"There's no limit to what a willing mind can do."

"More of your father's wisdom?"

"No, I think I got that from one of my books. Maybe it was Churchill, I don't know."

She liked it that he was well-read. Given the fact that her life had been dedicated to science, he probably had a broader general knowledge than she. In a strange way, that gave her comfort.

"Well," Brady said, "I guess I'll be saying good-night. I've got to get your chair out of the car and be on my way."

She held out her hand and he took it, holding her fingers. For a moment she let the connection be her statement, but then she said, "Thanks for today, Brady. It was a gift, a wonderful gift. I very much appreciate it . . . and everything else you've done." She squeezed her teddy bear against her breast.

"This is really beginning to feel like goodbye," he said.

She nodded.

"Strangely painful for such a new friendship."

She nodded again. Brady peered down at her. She wasn't sure if his eyes were getting glossy, but hers were.

"You know what?" she said. "I'm going to end up sleeping with this damned teddy bear for the next six months."

He squeezed the fingers he still held. "Is that the extent of your attention span?"

Her lip quivered. "I guess so."

"I'd be flattered if you remember me that long."

"I'll remember you longer," she whispered. A tear ran out of the corner of her eye and she wiped it away.

"I expect I'd better head out of here before we both start getting sentimental." He gave her a broad smile, but there was nostalgia in his eyes.

Sitting on the bed beside her, he leaned down and kissed her tenderly. "You take care of yourself, you hear?"

She nodded, biting her lip. Brady tweaked her nose and got up.

"Drop me a postcard and let me know how things are going," he said over his shoulder as he made his way to the door.

"Brady..."

He stopped and turned. "Ma'am?"

"Are you going to Big Sur tomorrow?"

"You made it sound awfully inviting."

"It is. My family has a cottage down there. I spent lots of summers there as a girl."

"Oh?"

"I could show it to you, if you're up to another day with a lady and her bear."

A big grin stretched across his face. "Now what self-respecting gentleman could turn down an offer like that?"

"You really want to?"

"I'll be here with bells on my toes."

"An early start, okay?"

"Say when."

"Nine?"

He chuckled. "California roosters sleep late."

"I'm not civil any earlier than that."

"How about ten?"

She gave him an admonishing look. "I'm not that bad."

"I'll be here at nine."

"I'll have Manuela make us a lunch. It's not exactly the time of year for picnics, but we'll manage."

"Sugar, we'll more than manage." With that he winked and left the room.

IT WAS DARK IN HER bedroom when Jane awoke. She glanced at the clock. It was eight-thirty, but seemed later. She'd slept for an hour and a half and she felt a real contentment. That was unusual, especially of late. If she'd been dreaming, she didn't know about what. But Brady was immediately in her thoughts, just as he had been when she'd dropped off to sleep.

It was amazing how quickly they'd established rapport. That didn't normally happen in new relationships. It probably had to do with her emotional vulnerability. She'd been susceptible to Jeremy, and was probably just as susceptible to Brady. That in itself was reason enough not to put a lot of stock in what had happened.

If that was her excuse, what was his? She'd been taken by him, but he'd been taken by her. The tenderness and affection he'd shown her was a good indicator of that. Plus, she'd felt the vibrations between them. They were sexual, yes, but there was deep emotion, as well.

She wondered, however, if Brady's strong feelings were really aimed at her. The purpose of his trip was to spare another poor woman his sister's fate. He'd said as much. Could the tenderness he felt for her be an extension of his feelings for Leigh?

Jane sighed. Ironically, she was making the same mistake with Brady that she'd made with Jeremy—letting her emotions run away with her. She'd been reaching out. The way she'd invited herself to go with him to Big Sur was proof of that. He'd been pleased, to be sure, but had she done either of them a favor? Probably not. She'd just prolonged their parting. Succumbed to the emotion of the moment.

Normally it wouldn't have been the end of the world, but in this case it was pretty silly to get embroiled with one man while still trying to untangle the mess she'd gotten into with another. Jeremy was her immediate problem, and he should be her immediate concern. She'd let his absence affect her—and, for that matter, she'd allowed Brady to take advantage of it.

Except for her second conversation with Bobby Dalton, nothing had really changed since Jeremy had left. Brady wasn't objective. For all she knew, Bobby Dalton wasn't, either. After all, he and Brady had known each other for years.

When she stopped to think about it, she was amazed how clear things could become after a little sleep, after a person stepped back from the emotion of the moment and took a good, hard look.

There was a soft rap on the door just then and it opened a crack, allowing light in from the hall. She could see Manuela's slender silhouette against the bright backdrop.

"*Señorita*," the housekeeper called softly, "are you awake?"

"Yes, Manuela, I'm awake," she replied.

"Excuse me for disturbing you, Doctor," the woman whispered as she approached the bed, "but Señor Trent, he is here."

"*Jeremy's* here?" Jane asked, shocked.

"Yes, *señorita*. He told me that he was worried for you and came on the first plane. He seems very upset and he wanted that I see if you are awake."

Jane was caught completely by surprise. It even frightened her a little. Then she heard Jeremy's voice in the hallway.

"Jane . . ."

She saw him through the half-open door. He peered into the darkness of the room.

"Yes, Jeremy," she called to him. "I was napping, but I'm awake now."

He was in the doorway, but he turned to the side, so as not to be intrusive. "I'm sorry to disturb you, darling, but I had to see you."

"Turn on the lamp, would you, Manuela?" she said, drawing up the throw covering her body.

The housekeeper stepped over and turned on the bedside lamp, casting a warm glow through the room. Jeremy looked in at her from the doorway. Concern was etched on his face.

"Forgive me for barging in this way," he said, "but I've been upset ever since we talked on the phone. I decided I had to come immediately."

Jane didn't recall him sounding that way during their conversation. "I'm not sure why you're upset," she said.

Jeremy, who was in a dark suit and tie, took a few steps into the room, glancing at Manuela. Jane realized he wanted privacy.

"Thank you, Manuela," she said. "You needn't stay."

"Is there something I can get you, Doctor?"

"Perhaps some tea. Jeremy, will you have tea with me?"

"Sure, if you like."

Manuela went off, leaving the door ajar. Jeremy stepped over and closed it. Jane felt a tremor of uncertainty. In her mind, he was no longer the man he'd been, certainly not the man with whom she'd shared her bed only a few nights ago.

Turning, he smiled for the first time. "I can't tell you how good it is to see you, darling," he said.

"It's good to see you, too, Jeremy."

He slowly made his way to the bed. Jane felt her heart pick up its beat. She searched his face, looking for a clue to his state of mind. The face that she'd always regarded as kind and sympathetic had a somber look about it; the normally smooth brow was slightly furrowed.

"You've made a friend in my absence," he said. His tone wasn't exactly accusatory, but it was solemn.

"A friend?"

Jeremy pointed at the teddy bear beside her, a crooked smile touching his lips.

"Oh," Jane said, taking the bear and holding it against her. "Yes, this is my new friend."

"Funny, the things you discover about a person after you get to know them." He sat down beside her, just where Brady had sat only a few hours earlier. He took her hand.

"I went to my office today," she said. "There were some stuffed animals there and I brought this one home."

"Then I shouldn't feel jealous."

She shook her head. "No, nothing to be jealous about."

Jeremy leaned over to kiss her and she turned her head slightly, offering him her cheek. His lips were cool.

"I'm surprised you decided to go to your office," he said. "I thought you were going to wait until you could walk again."

"I decided I needed to get out. My intent was to visit, but Joan Bosche was alone and the place was full of sick babies. The next thing I knew I was treating patients."

"I just hope you didn't push yourself. Your health must come first. There are other doctors to take care of the sick."

It annoyed her a little that he was making a negative out of what she'd considered to be a positive experience. But then, he always had struck her as conservative. Before, she'd regarded his attitude toward her as caring and concerned; now she wondered if he didn't prefer her dependent, even ineffectual.

"It doesn't please you that I say that," he observed.

He'd always been good at reading her. She'd noticed that from the first. Initially she'd regarded it as an indication of his perceptiveness, a sign of rapport. Now she wasn't so sure.

He was rubbing her fingers as he looked into her eyes. Jane looked back at him, asking herself who this man was. Was Jeremy showing compassion and understanding, or was he the diabolical man Brady Coleman had made him out to be? It took an effort not to recoil.

"Does it displease you, Jane?" he asked, repeating his question.

"Oh, no. Of course not. You've always been concerned about me. I respect that about you," she replied.

"But something is wrong. I can see it."

His tone was superficially gentle, but he was clearly suspicious. Or was it her? Was she feeling guilty for having been disloyal?

Her instinct was to put all her cards on the table, but she was afraid. Whether the stories about him were true or not, the risk of a confrontation seemed great. She felt inadequate and vulnerable. Only then did she realize that it was her weakness that Jeremy played on. He had from the very first.

"Jane?"

She scooted up, propping a pillow against the headboard, putting a little distance between them. "Yes, you're right," she said. "There is something wrong."

"What?"

She drew a calming breath. "I've decided I can't wear your ring," she said, holding up her bare finger. "It's too early in our relationship."

Jeremy nodded. "I figured that's what it was. That's why I rushed back here. I upset you by pushing things and, believe me, darling, that's the very last thing I wanted to do." He reached out and touched her cheek. "You mean too much to me."

"No permanent harm done," she said, feeling better, sensing that she'd gained some measure of control. "We just need to take a big step back."

"Of course," he said. "Whatever you wish is fine with me. But promise me you'll keep an open mind about the future."

"You're talking like asking me to marry you is a sin, Jeremy. I don't want you to think that's how I feel. I was flattered. But I haven't been myself since the accident. You haven't known the real me. I'm much stronger and more complete than the person you've known. I'm more the way I was today when I was in my office, doing my work."

He studied her. It was difficult to tell what he was thinking, but she did know he wasn't overjoyed by her words.

"You aren't pleased that I say that, are you?" she ventured.

"Why do you say that?"

She couldn't tell him the truth. "You've only known me as a invalid," she said. "You're having trouble relating to me as a competent, self-sufficient person."

"That's not true," he said, shaking his head. "I want only one thing for you, Jane. I want you to be happy."

Why didn't that ring true? Why was she inclined to believe Brady—a man she barely knew? How could she have been so blind the past few months?

Jeremy looked pained. "There's something else," he said. "There's something more you haven't mentioned."

She bolstered herself as best she could. "What happened in your first two marriages has upset me," she confessed.

"I was rather curt when you asked about Leigh on the phone. I didn't think that was the time or place to discuss her. If I was abrasive, I apologize."

"No, it wasn't that...."

"Then what?"

She swallowed hard. "Jeremy, please tell me what happened to Leigh." She looked him in the eye. "I want the unvarnished truth. If ever there was a time for candor, it's now. I don't care how bad it may look."

His mouth formed a tight line. He got up and went to the window where he stared out at the darkness. Manuela knocked on the door and Jane called for her to enter. The housekeeper was carrying a tray holding Jane's grandmother's silver tea service.

"Just put it down on the table," Jane said.

Manuela did as she'd asked. "Do you need anything else, *señorita?*"

"No, the tea's fine. Thank you."

Manuela glanced at Jeremy, then quietly left the room. Jane turned her attention back to him. She could see his reflection in the glass. Somehow she knew what he was about to say would be pivotal.

He slowly turned around. "My marriages ended tragically, as you know, Jane. What I probably haven't conveyed to you is the great sorrow I bear because of it. And the guilt."

"Guilt?"

"Yes. Both tragedies could have been avoided. It was within my power to have prevented what happened, and I didn't. I failed them. Leigh and Victoria, both."

"How so?"

He began recounting the story she'd already heard from Brady and Bobby Dalton, with certain details omitted. Jeremy paced as he talked. "I was the one who left the bedroom window unlocked, and I allowed the intruder to overpower me. He was smaller and older. It shouldn't have happened.

"As for Victoria, I didn't appreciate the darkness of her mood, nor did I investigate how many pills she'd taken. I made her a drink when the responsible thing would have been to refuse. Those are my sins, Jane, and I shall carry the burden of them to my grave."

He stopped then and looked at her from the foot of the bed.

"In either case, did the police suspect you of wrong-doing?" she asked. "Were you investigated?"

There was questioning on his face, a flash of uncertainty.

"There were the usual questions, of course. In the minds of the police, no one is above suspicion."

"Jeremy," she said in a level tone, "my lawyer is already checking into your background. It seemed the prudent thing to do. I know about the scratches and the fact that particles of your flesh were found under Leigh's fingernails."

A dark look crossed his face. "Then this conversation has been a test. You set a trap."

"I'm merely being cautious. I have to know."

He was silent for a long time, then he said, "I haven't wanted to be critical of either Leigh or Victoria, because they can't defend themselves, but now my reputation is on the line, not to mention our future together."

"That isn't my intent."

"Don't sugarcoat it," he said pointedly. "You want a candid conversation, so let me be direct. Did your investigator report that Leigh was emotionally disturbed, under the care of a psychiatrist? Did he happen to mention what Leigh's complaints about me were?"

Jane lowered her eyes.

"No, I didn't think so. She couldn't accept me as I am, Jane, that was her principal complaint. She married me, but she wasn't happy when I wasn't like the rough-and-tumble Texans she'd grown up with—men who showed their affection by playing rough. *She* was the one who dictated the conditions of our sex life, not I.

"The night she died, she attacked me in the middle of our lovemaking, trying to provoke me into the violence that turned her on. And as for Victoria, I believe I've already told you her problems. They're well-known by everyone. She was under the continual care of doctors months before I met her."

"Jeremy," she said, "I'm not accusing you of anything."

He ignored the comment. "I may not have handled either situation well, but I didn't intentionally hurt anyone. If I sinned, they were sins of omission. That I swear to you!"

His tone had gotten progressively sharper. She could see that he was upset.

"There have been allegations," he went on more calmly. "Especially by Leigh's brother. He hated me and I didn't much care for him. And it's possible the prosecutor may have bought into some of his unproved charges. The two of them are boyhood friends. All that truly matters is the person I am, the person you know, Jane. Have you ever seen even the slightest hint of violence in me?"

She looked down at her folded hands. "No."

"Then trust the man you know," he implored. "I can't blame you for being skeptical. But the truth is on my side. And so is the law. Don't condemn me on the basis of rumor and innuendo."

She looked up at him. She could see the intensity of his emotion. "That's only fair," she admitted. "You're right."

"Then you'll give me a chance?"

"Yes," she said softly. "But I still can't wear your ring. Not yet. I want you to take it back until the time is right."

"I'd rather you keep it, even if you won't wear it."

She shook her head. "No. It'll mean more if it's done right." She took it out of the drawer in the nightstand and held it out for him to take.

Jeremy returned to the side of the bed and sat down. His eyes were liquid with emotion. He took the ring and slipped it into his pocket. "I regard this as only a temporary setback."

She nodded. Jeremy looked very sad. And she had to admit, he looked innocent, as well. She had believed Brady, and still did. She had no doubt about his sincerity, but she had to admit that it was possible he had been misled by his own passion, the intensity of his dislike for Jeremy. Each of them, in their own way, could be telling the truth.

Jeremy reached out and touched her arm. "Manuela said you were tired. I'm afraid my visit has added to your burdens. I'll leave and let you get your rest. But if you trust nothing else, Jane, trust this. I love you. I love you very much."

He leaned over and kissed her lightly on the lips. Then he looked back and forth between her eyes, his expression imploring. Once again Jeremy was the man she'd known, the one who'd first come to her rescue. Now, though, she regarded him with caution.

He touched her cheek with his fingertips a last time, then went to the door. Sincere or false, it was an inspiring performance. But there was one thing that had gone unasked.

"Jeremy," she called to him.

He turned. "Yes, darling?"

"Did Victoria like rough sex, too?"

He seemed to be knocked off-balance by the question. He hesitated, then said, "Why, no. Why do you ask?"

"Did you have rough sex with her the night she lapsed into the coma?"

He shifted uneasily. "When Victoria was under the influence of drugs and alcohol she could get irrational, even violent. But that's not what you're talking about, is it?"

She shook her head. "No, I guess it isn't."

"What were you getting at?"

She waved off the question. "I was curious, that's all."

He didn't understand, but seemed to sense it wasn't important. He left her then, sitting alone in silence. After several moments, tears bubbled up and overflowed Jane's lids. She wiped them away. It was all terribly painful. But there was something else, something she could not deny. Deep in her soul, she was frightened—frightened in a way she'd never been before.

9

SOMETIME DURING the middle of the night the wind came up. Jane listened to it rustling the trees and whistling around the eaves. At first she worried about Brady and Jeremy. Then she realized this wasn't only about them—it was about her. She didn't know who she truly was. Ironic as it seemed, she was in search of herself.

She awoke to the realization that a late-winter storm had moved in. It wouldn't be a good day for an outing, although the coast was never more beautiful than when it was being lashed by wind and rain. She'd leave it up to Brady if he wanted to see Big Sur under those conditions. Meanwhile, she had to get up and get ready to greet him.

After considering what to wear, she had Manuela dig an old pair of jeans and a flannel shirt from the back of her closet. She hadn't worn either in years, but they seemed a fitting tribute to Brady, one she suspected he would appreciate. Curiously, she felt the need to please him, which in itself was interesting.

As she dressed, Jane tried to stand with Manuela's help, testing her legs, but they were too weak. She was disappointed because she badly wanted tangible proof that she would recover the use of her legs. Her hunger for normalcy suddenly seemed more intense than ever.

"What if I never walk again?" she said.

"You will, *señorita*. It takes time, no? You are only now starting to use your legs."

Jane knew that, but she needed reassurance anyway. She was like a child in that respect. Deep down she wondered whether her doubts had anything to do with her legs at all. Maybe something more profound than that was at issue.

After they'd finished breakfast, there was still time before Brady was due to arrive, so Jane asked Manuela to build a fire to cheer the house. It was the perfect antidote for a cold, rainy day and her mood.

For fifteen minutes she sat by the fire, listening to piano sonatas, fighting her nervousness. It made no sense that Brady's imminent arrival should put her in such a state. When the phone rang she thought it was he, but instead it was Melissa Krum.

"I got a preliminary report from the investigators I hired," Melissa began. "I thought you might like to be updated."

"By all means."

"Let's start with Mr. Trent," she said. "My man in Connecticut talked with his ex-wife's family. It isn't good, Jane. They claim Mr. Trent was after his wife's money right from the start. And they're deeply suspicious about the accident that put her in a coma. The son flatly said they were able to force a favorable financial settlement by agreeing to use their influence to stifle the criminal investigation."

"Good Lord. You're saying Jeremy bought his way out of trouble."

"That's their story," Melissa said. "Who knows how objective they are. It's safe to say the family saw Trent as an adversary and didn't want him running off with their inheritance. In fairness, the issue could be money as much as wrongdoing."

"Everybody I talk to about Jeremy seems to have an ax to grind. How does a person ever get the truth?"

"We keep digging. The detective is trying to get what he can from the police. I'll have an update in a couple of days."

Jane felt sick. "What about Brady?"

"Mr. Coleman is a man of a different color. He seems to be living on the edge as far as business goes. He has considerable debts and numerous unhappy creditors."

"He as good as told me that already. Anything else?"

"The investigator's comment was that Mr. Coleman has more success with the ladies than with drilling oil wells."

"That's not a surprise, either."

"There'll be more later," Melissa said. "I asked for a preliminary report and I wanted to pass along the little I got."

"Thanks. Let me know if anything hot turns up." Jane hung up, realizing she hadn't really learned anything new other than the fact that the families of *both* of Jeremy's ex-wives didn't have a very high regard for him."

She pulled her chair closer to the crackling fire. She shivered, but more because of her anxiety than the dampness.

After a few minutes she heard a car in the drive. It was a couple of minutes after nine, so it had to be Brady. She was glad. The man was confounding. He'd upset her life, made her question and doubt everything she'd been clinging to, and yet something about him made her happy and eager for his company.

Manuela greeted Brady at the door. Jane heard the same cheerful chatter as the day before. She waited with growing excitement until he and Manuela came into the great room, both smiling. He was in his sheepskin coat, but unlike the previous times, he had on a cowboy hat, as well. His rugged good looks had a powerful effect on her. They stared at each other for a moment, then Brady removed his hat and made his way toward her.

"Morning, sugar," he said amiably. Reaching her side, he knelt down next to her chair and took her hand. "You look as pretty as bluebonnet on a shiny spring morning."

"My, Brady, more flowers? I look like bluebonnet and smell like a yellow rose of Texas?"

"Well, let's see about the rose part." He embraced her, pressing his cold face into her neck, nuzzling her.

"Hey, you're cold!" she protested, giggling.

"Yep, sweetest rose I ever did smell."

"And you're nothin' but a sweet-talkin' man," she teased, affecting his accent. "Bet you used that line a hundred times."

He smiled with amusement. "Darlin', the only issue is sincerity, and I couldn't be more sincere."

"Probably said that before, too."

"You're one of the fairest blossoms I've ever known, sugar, but not the only one."

"So I hear."

He gave her a questioning look.

"Your reputation precedes you."

"The good as well as the bad, I hope."

"There's good, too?" He pinched her in the ribs, making her squeal. "Stop that! I hate to be tickled!"

Brady laughed. She ran her eyes over his face. Any tentativeness she'd felt before his arrival had dissipated. She was even happier to see him than she'd expected.

"Looks like we've got some weather this morning," he said, brushing the moisture from the shoulders of his coat. "If you don't mind, I'll take this off."

"No, please do."

Brady got to his feet.

"Put on your hat again," she said. "It's the first time I've seen you in the whole . . . outfit."

He chuckled and put the hat back on, tilting it down over one eye in a roguish fashion. "Umbrellas aren't the apparel of choice on a ranch," he said. "A hat's the best way to keep the rain off your head."

She examined him admiringly. "You look pretty authentic, Mr. Coleman, I must admit."

"I see you've got on your country best this mornin'."

"But no hat, I'm afraid."

He slipped off his coat and removed his hat again. "I'll send you one as soon as I get home. There's nothing so pathetic as a half-baked cowpoke."

"I'm not sure Calamity Jane is the real me," she replied. "But thanks for the thought.

He checked her out more thoroughly. "Your outfit's pretty good, actually, though the sneakers need rethinking."

He gave her a sly wink and dropped into a nearby chair, glancing at the fire. "We've got an appreciation for this in common," he said, gesturing toward the flames. "Nothing like a crackling fire to warm the spirit."

"How true. Nothing's more inviting on a day like this."

They both gazed at the flames.

"I was wondering if you'd be having second thoughts about going down to Big Sur, given the weather."

"Would you rather not go?" he asked.

"I'll do whatever you want. But I have to warn you, the coast won't be at its best."

"The easy thing would be to sit here by this fire, I grant you. But I've got a streak in my soul that cries for adventure. I've seen the seeds of that in you, too, Jane. Maybe you need to set caution aside and push yourself a little."

"You're right," she said. "After yesterday, I've learned there's no need to hold back. That was your gift to me."

The comment pleased him, she could tell. "So, where does that leave us? Do we saddle up?"

"Sure. If you want to, I'll brave the storm."

"Let's get goin' then, shall we?"

Jane nodded. "Yes, but I want to tell you something first."

He settled back in his chair. "What's that?"

"Jeremy came back last night."

A dark look crossed Brady's face. "Oh?"

"Yes. He was concerned after our phone conversation and got an earlier flight. We had a long talk."

Brady's expression was more one of displeasure than concern.

"I didn't say I'd seen you," she said, "but I asked some probing questions."

"And?"

"He seemed to have an answer for everything."

"That doesn't surprise me," Brady groused. "J.T.'s as slippery as they come."

"I don't know about that, but I gave him back his ring. I haven't ended the relationship, but I put it on hold."

"Pending?"

"The independent investigation I'm conducting."

He nodded approvingly. "I knew you just needed your eyes opened. I'm glad you're taking the cautious approach."

"I have you to thank for that, Brady. I'm grateful."

"I aim to please."

"I might as well tell you I'm checking you out, too. I saw no reason to be cautious about Jeremy and fool-hardy about you."

Brady hesitated. "You're nothing if you aren't consistent, darlin'. Any juicy tidbits I ought to know about?"

"Nothing you haven't told me one way or another."

"That's a relief."

"I don't have to worry about surprises, then?" she asked.

"When I was just knee-high to a grasshopper my daddy told me a man can gamble at cards, he can gamble at business, he can even gamble with women, but there's no percentage in gamblin' with the truth. I've found from experience it's a low-stress way to live."

"An admirable philosophy."

"My daddy was poor, but he wasn't stupid."

"And it sounds like he was happy."

Brady pondered the remark. "He was, for the most part. But before he died he made a confession. He told me if he had it to do over again he'd have played his hand with my mother differently. 'The ladies are a pleasure when you're young,' he said, 'but when you're old and you don't have someone to love and be loved by, your freedom starts seemin' mighty insignificant.'"

Jane wondered if he was trying to tell her something. "How do you feel about that?"

"It's made old age seem less appealing—let me put it that way."

Jane laughed. "You're so full of it, Brady Coleman, I don't know when to believe you and when I shouldn't."

"I try to maintain a little mystery," he said. "Every man needs a gimmick. Mine is being truthful in an unorthodox way."

"Unorthodox is the best description I've heard of you yet."

"Let's just hope it works."

Jane wasn't sure exactly what he meant and decided it was best not to ask. Brady got to his feet.

"What do you think, little lady? Shall we go tweak Mother Nature on the nose?"

His good humor lifted her spirits and she laughed again. "Why not?"

Manuela brought Jane her ski parka and Brady carried her to the car. It was hardly an ideal way to interact with a man but, in his arms, she did have a special feeling. Jane couldn't help wondering if it wasn't a little too comfortable for her own good.

After Brady got her chair and the picnic lunch that Manuela had made for them packed into the car, they took off. They drove to the Coast Highway in a light rain, although out to sea the sky was very dark and the storm seemed to be intensifying.

Heading south, they passed Carmel, Point Lobos and Notleys Landing. The road rose higher into the mists, twisting along the edge of the great cliff that dominated that section of the coast. Brady drove carefully. Jane watched the storm through the sweep of the windshield wipers.

"Have you ever come close to marrying?" she asked, after a long silence.

"Not really."

"Was it because you never loved a woman that way, or because you couldn't conscience the idea of settling down?"

"Probably a little of both. I wasn't looking for the right girl, and the right girl didn't come along. I've always figured it was meant to be that way."

"In other words, you haven't lost any sleep over it."

"No, ma'am."

Jane smiled. His directness was refreshing.

"How about you?" he asked.

"You won't like hearing this, but Jeremy was the first man I thought I might love. I was still playing with the idea when all this came up. I hadn't really come to any conclusions."

"You mean of all the fellas who surely chased after you over the years, not one turned your head?"

"I noticed men. I even cared for a few along the way. But none of them seemed as important to me as my career. I took that to be significant. I decided if someone was meant to be special, I'd discover it. So I didn't worry about it."

"Maybe you and I have more in common than meets the eye," he said. "Sounds like we've been going down parallel ruts in the same trail."

"You think if you'd had an accident like I did, the girl who nursed you back to health might have snagged you?"

Brady slowed the car to negotiate a big hairpin curve. Even after they were past it, he didn't answer right away. "I hadn't quite thought of it in those terms," he finally said, "but in a manner of speaking I did have my accident."

"What do you mean?"

"When I lost Leigh."

That hadn't occurred to her, but when she stopped to think about it, it made sense. "So, what you're saying is that we're both wounded souls."

Brady chuckled. "Yeah. Two wounded souls goin' out for a picnic in the middle of a rainstorm."

"It's different, you must admit."

He nodded. "I think that's what I like about it."

After several more miles of spectacular views of the gray, roiling sea and foamy breakers on the rocks, they came to Point Sur state park.

"Is this where we'll find the picnic table?" he asked.

"I think we need plan *B*, unless you're more of a masochist than I am."

"Any ideas?"

"We could just drive around looking at the sights, then eat in the car when we get hungry. "Or," she added, "we could go to my family's cottage. It's been over a year since I've been there and I have no idea what condition it's in."

"Does it have a view?"

"A spectacular view. And a fireplace," she said, provocatively.

He gave her a wry look. "Tell me the truth. Was that in the back of your mind when we were sitting by the fire at your place this morning?"

Jane flushed despite herself. "In the back of my mind, maybe."

His grin turned sly. "You're a woman after my own heart, sugar."

"I hope you mean that as a compliment."

"Is the pope Catholic?"

Jane gave him a sideward glance, then pointed up the highway. "There's a road running off to the right about three miles up. That's where we'll turn."

BRADY OCCASIONALLY glanced at her as they drove along the narrow, semipaved road. He was feeling good, happier than he had in years. Courting came as naturally to him as breathing. It had been that way from the day he'd first noticed girls.

If he could seduce a woman and please her as well as satisfy himself, he'd do it without a second thought. That was the way life worked. But this relationship with Jane Stewart didn't fit the mold. It was not that sort of thing; yet he couldn't clearly say what it was.

Jane was different and his feelings toward her were different, but he struggled to understand why, and what that meant. He felt a certain compassion for her that was normally not a part of his relationship with a woman. If and when he started feeling a bit soft-hearted, he would normally back off. But compassion—even the responsibility he felt toward Jane—did not fully explain what was going on. It was more than her situation that he was reacting to. It was her. When he looked into her eyes, he felt a tug, and not just the tug of physical desire. He felt a warmth and a caring that was all but alien to him.

Years earlier, Brady had stood with Jerry Branson when he'd married Laureline. He remembered how unreal it had all seemed, how empty and meaningless the minister's words. "To have and to hold . . . to cherish . . . until death do you part."

Cherish? What did that mean? Desire? Yes, he could relate to that. Even sharing made sense to him. A man gave a little to get a little.

And when Leigh had married Jeremy Trent, Brady had listened to the vows. "With this ring I incorporate thy assets." That's what he really heard when Jeremy had said his vows. Leigh, for her part, was a dreamer, a silly romantic. A child.

Brady knew he was cynical, although he liked to think of himself as being a realist, too. For him the issue was very simple. Either a person was honest or they weren't. He could say, "Darlin' I can't think of a thing I'd rather do than hold you in my arms and kiss those lips," and mean every last word of it. "I like bein' with you. I love your body. Sweetheart, you turn me on." All that was straightforward, easy to say, and easy to understand. That's what being a man who appreciated women was all about.

But when he looked at Jane, none of that applied and yet it all applied, though not in the way it always had. *Cherish.* That word kept popping into his head. "To have, to hold, to cherish." It made sense for the first time in his life. He wondered if that's what love meant.

"Turn into that drive," Jane said, pointing.

Brady left the lane they were on and followed two graveled ruts around the flank of a hill. They'd been in a forest since leaving the highway, but occasionally they'd broken into the open and were presented with spectacular views of misty, wooded gorges or a glimpse of the coastline. He knew the general direction was toward the sea, as the highway had gone inland after they'd left Point Sur.

They were several hundred feet above sea level, and clouds hung just above them. The rain continued to fall steadily.

"On a sunny day this place is incredibly beautiful," Jane lamented. "I wish you were seeing it at its best."

Brady reached over and covered her hand. "It's the company I care about."

A tiny smile touched her lips. *Cherish*, he thought. Yes, he did understand cherish.

The drive ended at a graveled parking area bordered by a semicircle of wooden posts. A path continued from there across the grassy slope. Fifty yards to the right was a precipice that evidently dropped to the sea. Farther up the slope, at the edge of a wood crowning the hilltop, was the cottage. It was only partially visible from the parking area where Brady brought the car to a stop.

"My father didn't want automobiles to ruin the look," Jane explained, "so he ended the drive here. As kids, my sister and I thought it was silly to have to trudge all that way up the hill with our suitcase or groceries or whatever when we could as easily drive." She stared off wistfully as Brady watched her. "What I wouldn't give now to be able to walk up to that door," she added.

"You will again, Jane."

"Yes, I hope so."

He wiped the steamed-up windshield with his hand. "Looks like the path might be a bit too muddy for your chair," he said. "I think you'd best ride up there piggyback."

"Oh, that's silly," she said. "I should have thought of the difficulty of getting me up there. Let's eat here in the car. We still can enjoy the view."

"No," he insisted. "We've come this far. Not going on would be like stopping drilling a well just because you ran into an unexpected rock stratum the last hundred feet. We've got to see this through."

"*No* is not a word you like, is it, Brady?"

"Am I being too hard?"

"Yes, but I kind of like it. My father was tough-minded that way, too. He used to infuriate me at times, but he was so often right I couldn't fault him."

"I think I'll take that as a compliment."

"You wouldn't be far wrong."

Brady grabbed his hat from the back seat and went around to the passenger side of the car and opened the door. He squatted down and looked into her gray eyes. "You really don't mind goin' piggyback, sweet pea?"

"Whatever's easiest for you, Brady. *You're* having to be the beast of burden."

"If you promise not to use your spurs, playin' horsey's probably easiest."

"Okay, Trigger, let's go."

Brady turned his back to her, leaning close to the car. "Put your arms around my neck and I'll lift you right out."

Jane did as he asked. Standing, he lifted her right out of the car and scooted her up on his back so that her legs were wrapped around his waist. He grasped them.

"How's that?" he asked.

"My legs feel limp as rags."

"They need a little firming up, that's all." He gave them a squeeze.

"A *lot* of firming up," she replied.

"Maybe we should go dancing."

"Yeah, sure."

Brady started up the path. The rain began to fall more heavily. The footing was tricky and he had to be careful. The last thing he needed was to take a header with her on his back. Of course, rolling around in the grass could be fun, even if it was wet.

"Ever go skinny-dippin' in the rain?" he asked.

"No, can't say that I have. Bet you have, though."

"One New Year's Eve when I was sixteen some friends of mine and I went down to Concepcion Park in San Antonio. It had been raining for two or three days and San Pedro Creek was up. It ran right along the park. After we'd each had a six-pack, we decided it was time to go for a little swim.

"To make a long story short, the police fished five drunk teenagers out of the drink, letting us spend the night in jail. My stepfather refused to bail me out until the last bowl game was over the next day, knowin' that seein' the A&M game was more important to me than anything on earth."

"Forgive me, but it sounds to me like you got just what you deserved."

He laughed. "I know your type, Lady Jane. You were one of those Goody Two-Shoes who studied all the time, never rebelled, kept the top button of her blouse closed at all times and thought she'd go to hell if a boy got his tongue in her mouth."

"You say it with such disdain, Brady, I venture to say you were rejected once by just such a girl."

"More than once."

"And you've been taking it out on womankind ever since?"

"Careful, missy, you're ridin' on my legs. It's no time to get uppity."

"What are you saying? That you'd dump me right here on the hillside in the rain?"

"Seems I do have the leverage to exact any favor I please."

"Oh, God, what a time to discover I've been carried off by a pervert."

"Guess you have no alternative but to be nice, sugar."

The path got steeper and Brady had to concentrate on what he was doing. By the time they made it to the large covered porch running the width of the cottage, he was winded.

"Whew!" he said, trudging up the steps and out of the rain at last. "To justify that, we may have to stay a day or two."

"It's downhill back to the car, Buffalo Bill."

"Does that mean I can roll you back?"

"Very funny!"

Brady carefully lowered her to the deck, turning to grasp her as she clung to his jacket. He clamped his arms around her waist, holding her to him. Jane looked into his eyes. "What are you thinking?" she asked.

"Oh, nothing."

"Nothing?"

"I was thinkin' you look so delicious that I ought to invite you to dance right now."

"If you let go of me, I'd slither to the floor like a wet noodle, Brady."

"Guess I better keep a good grip then, shouldn't I, darlin'?"

Their faces were inches apart. He felt like kissing Jane now. Before he could, though, she turned her face up to his, inviting him to cover her mouth. He did so without hesitation, kissing her deeply.

He felt his heart lurch and he had a tremendous desire for her. But it wasn't just sexual. It was more complex than that. As they kissed, the rain started coming down in a torrent, thundering on the roof.

When their lips finally parted, he kissed the end of her nose. "I expect I better get you inside before you melt."

Jane turned her head toward the door. "Oh, damn," she said over the roar of the rain.

"What's the matter?"

"The door key is in my purse and my purse is in the car."

Brady rolled his eyes, then looked down toward the parking area. The downpour was so heavy he could barely make out the silhouette of the car. And it had gotten darker, even though it was not yet midday.

"If you'd like to roll up in a ball, I'll be glad to give you a shove in the right direction," he chided.

"I'm sorry."

"Well, I knew I'd be goin' back for the lunch basket anyway. No reason to complain."

"We can sit and wait until it lets up," she said, nodding toward the bench against the front of the house.

"No, you're already wet. I'd better get you in out of the cold. Hope you have a few towels inside."

"I'm sure there'll be something we can use to dry off with."

"Shall I set you on the bench?"

"Yes, I guess so."

He started to pick her up to carry her over, then he thought better of it. "Since we're already in position, care to dance a bit?" he asked.

"Brady, it's all I can do to lift my foot off the ground."

"Stand on my toes," he said, lifting her and settling her back down so that her weight rested on his feet. He grasped her firmly around the waist with his right arm, then held her right hand in his left. "Do you sing?"

"I hum," she replied.

"Give us a few bars of 'Singing in the Rain,' why don't you?"

Jane laughed. "Brady Coleman, you're crazy."

He kissed her chin, then began two-stepping around the porch, to a verse of "Singing in the Rain," followed by "The Yellow Rose of Texas." After they'd danced for a minute or two he stopped and looked down at her. "Bet that's a first."

She nodded, looking surprisingly sad. Her eyes were even a bit glossy.

"What's the matter?" he asked.

"I used to do that with my father when I was a little girl. He was a wonderful dancer."

"Didn't mean to bring back any painful memories."

"Melancholy, not painful," she said. "Actually, it was nice."

He lifted her into his arms and carried her to the bench where he set her down, then sat beside her. He took her hand and rubbed it. "You be all right?"

"I'll be fine."

Brady got to his feet and tousled her wet hair. "Okay. I'll be back in a few minutes."

He went to the top of the steps and stopped. He looked back at her. Then pushing his hat farther down on his brow, Brady pivoted on his heel and went back out into the blowing rain.

10

JANE LAY ON THE BED in the alcove at the back of the living room, wrapped in a blanket. Brady had propped pillows behind her so she could watch him make a fire. Fortunately there had been a dozen pieces of dry wood stacked by the stone fireplace. He'd taken off his boots and left them outside the door because they were covered with mud and he said he didn't want to track up the house.

As he worked on building the fire to a hardy blaze, Jane noticed he had holes in the heels of both his socks. For some reason it touched her that poor Brady was running around with holes in his socks. It brought her cowboy down to more human proportions. Even though she was perfectly aware he was a flawed human being like every other, in her mind he did have a bigger-than-life quality about him—probably because he was such a physical man.

He left the fireplace and made his way back to the bed. Before sitting beside her, he looked down at the soaked legs of his jeans. "I suppose if I'm careful it won't hurt to sit down."

"That has to feel miserable. Why don't you take them off? I won't look."

Brady shook his head. "They'll dry faster if I keep them on. Besides, there's nothing as pathetic as a man with his pants off," he said. "Unless, of course, he has amorous intentions and means to prove his manhood."

Jane laughed at the comment and said, "Can't you handle the thought of being vulnerable occasionally? Isn't it all right to be weak or afraid or feel insecure and needy sometimes? Or does your self-respect require being macho all the time?"

"A man's biggest fear is failure," he replied. "From the time we're little boys we learn it's important to stay a step ahead of the game. That's why we're always measuring ourselves against each other. That's what sports are all about. Business, too, for that matter."

"Once again your perceptiveness surprises me, Brady."

"Pretty soon you'll start thinking I'm not a hick after all," he said with a wink. He picked up the towel he'd used to dry her hair earlier and dabbed her cheek.

At times his gentleness surprised her. Perhaps that was what made its effect on her so powerful. She looked into his eyes. "I've never thought of you as a hick."

"Oh, really?"

"Rough, perhaps, but that's different."

He ran the tip of his index finger along her jaw. "First impressions can be tricky. My first impression of you was that you were irascible," he said. "Pretty and irascible."

"How could you think those two things at the same time?"

"Oh, it's an appealing combination, believe me."

"You like irascible women, Brady?" She was incredulous.

"Irascible, but tamable," he replied.

"There's no sport in an easy conquest, is that it? No challenge to measure yourself against?"

He cuffed her affectionately. "Hey, you catch on quickly, don't you, sugar?"

"You know, it's a wonder women ever get taken in by men."

"Why's that?"

"Because you're all so full of bull...you-know-what. Not to mention egocentric."

Brady folded his arms over his chest and gave her a sideward glance. "In my experience hostility is a sign of deep yearnin'," he said easily. "You aren't feeling the same attraction for me I'm feelin' for you, are you?"

Jane blinked. She wasn't sure if he was teasing or if he intended the comment seriously. "That is not amusing."

"I didn't mean to be, sweet pea. I'm dead serious."

She stared at him blankly.

After several moments he said, "Shall I take your silence to mean yes, you *are* feeling the same attraction?"

She decided he was playing with her. She gave him a sharp jab with her elbow. "Any attraction I've felt has mercifully passed," she replied. "So don't worry about me attacking you."

He put his hand on her blanket-covered leg, rubbing it absently. "I probably shouldn't admit this," he said, "but you confound me. You've got me at a total loss."

"What do you mean by that?"

"I'm not sure how you make me feel, but something strange is happening in here," he said, touching his heart.

Jane searched his incredible blue eyes as the fire crackled. "You've only known me a few days and you're saying you feel something special?"

"I said strange, but it's special, too. It's only happened a few times in my life."

"Thanks, Brady. Do you say such nice things to all the girls?"

"No. I have this funny habit of saying what I really feel."

"I'm touched," she said. She slipped her fingers out from under her blanket and took his hand.

Brady looked down at her hand and seemed pleased. She sighed with contentment. The fire had warmed the cottage, which was actually beginning to feel homey.

With the atmosphere more relaxed, she allowed herself the luxury of looking around and conjuring up old memories of her childhood. The furniture was a hodgepodge of things her mother had collected over the years, comfortable old chairs and tables, a breakfront that had belonged to her grandmother.

In addition to the living room, there was a **bed**room and a loft. The bed had been placed in the alcove to accommodate extra guests. Jane had always liked it because she could be in bed and still see the ocean. Margaret had preferred the loft and, of course, her parents had always taken the bedroom when the family came down to Big Sur for weekends or during the summer. Since her parents had died, Jane had visited the cottage infrequently, usually when she wanted to be alone or felt nostalgic. When Brady caught her eye, she realized he'd been watching her.

"So, are you happy to be here in your old stompin' grounds?" he asked.

"I *was* remembering."

"Yeah, I could tell."

"It's nice to be here with you," she admitted with a frankness that surprised even her.

"I'm glad."

They gazed into each other's eyes for a long time.

"What are you thinking?" she asked, when he didn't seem inclined to share his thoughts.

"I was thinkin' you're the sweetest damn thing I've ever seen," he murmured.

"Why do you say that?"

"I suppose because it's true."

She had no idea if they were empty words—the sort of thing that men say—or if they were heartfelt. Brady appeared to understand her uncertainty because he took action to prove the point. Taking her chin, he lightly kissed her lips.

A tremor went through her, followed by the first twinges of excitement. After the kiss ended he brushed his cheek against hers and inhaled her scent. Jane swallowed hard. She'd been conscious of the physical man from the beginning, but never so strongly as now.

"This is sort of unexpected," she mumbled, feeling she had to say something.

"Is it?"

"I find you very attractive," she said. "But . . ."

"But what?"

"But this isn't . . . We shouldn't . . . Do you really . . ."

He kissed her nose. "You aren't makin' a lot of sense, sugar. Spit it out."

"What I'm trying to say is . . ."

"Yes?"

"This isn't appropriate."

"Why not? You're a girl and I'm a boy. Girls and boys do these sorts of things."

"Yes, but . . ."

"But what, darlin'?"

"Oh, Brady, why do you insist on making me say it?"

"Because I don't know what you're thinkin'. All I've heard is a bunch of hummin' and hawin'."

She gave him a look. "My intention is not to be seduced!" Her eyes flashed. "There! I said it. Do you understand, now?"

"Sure, I understand. But I don't believe it."

Jane's mouth dropped open. "What?"

"I understand, but I don't believe what you're sayin'. We didn't come up here for the view. That much I do know."

She shook her head in disbelief. "What incredible gall!"

"Well, why do *you* think we came up here?" he asked with an innocence that irked her to no end.

"To have a picnic lunch!"

"Well, yes," he said. "That, too."

She shook her head with exasperation. "You actually think I came here to be seduced? I can't believe this."

"If you were expectin' pity, you won't be gettin' it from me. We all have handicaps of one kind or another."

"Handicap? That's what you think this is about?"

"As far as I'm concerned you're a woman, same as any other."

"Except I make you feel strange here," she said, touching her heart.

"I hope you aren't makin' fun of me, Jane. I was utterly sincere when I told you that."

She was exasperated. "Brady, you're the most confounding man I've ever met!"

He gave her leg a squeeze through the blanket. "But do I turn you on? That's the question."

She whipped her head around toward him, ready to set him straight, tell him in no uncertain terms that sex was the very last thing she was interested in. She found him grinning, his eyes laughing at her, not mocking but full of delight. She frantically searched her brain for the perfect retort. All she could do, though, was stare.

Brady apparently took her reaction as an affirmative answer because he kissed her again, this time slipping his hand behind her head and firmly pressing his mouth to hers. She started to resist, but discovered she didn't want to. Turning, she grasped his broad shoulders and pressed her body as close to his as she could, tasting his mouth, savoring the sensuousness of his lips.

After the kiss ended she pressed her forehead against his, holding his head in her hands. "You bastard," she murmured.

"Why do you say that, sweetheart?"

"Because all you want is another notch in your gun belt—your first wheelchair case. And here I am, on the verge of accommodating you."

"You can't accept the fact that it might be you I'm interested in?"

She didn't answer. She was afraid to believe it was true. And she was embarrassed, too. She'd been dishonest. He was right. She *had* wanted to be seduced, although until now, this moment, she wouldn't have admitted it—even to herself.

"Is it me you're afraid of or your own feelings?" he asked gently.

Jane looked into his eyes. "You're so damned perceptive it's scary."

A little smile bent the corners of his mouth.

"Don't get too smug. Jeremy's the same way."

That brought a frown.

"But Jeremy perceives weakness. And pounces on it. I didn't realize that until you came along, Brady."

"What do *I* pounce on, pray tell?"

She considered the question, looking at the driving rain through the windows. "I don't know. Desire, maybe. But that's not all. There's more, but I'm not sure what."

He took her hand and rubbed the back of it with his thumb. "Maybe this is a time to feel and not think."

She smiled. "It's easy to see why you do so well with the ladies. I bet most of them want to please you as much as they want pleasure for themselves. You have that quality, you know. You make people—women—want to please you."

"I wouldn't know."

"You probably aren't even conscious of it."

"You're thinkin' again, darlin'."

She patted his cheek, looking into his guileless eyes, knowing he was a lady-killer, one who could make a woman die happy. "You really want to make love with a cripple?"

He wagged his finger admonishingly. "The first thing I ought to do, missy, is turn you over my knee and blister your butt. There's no cause for self-pity."

"Maybe it's self-doubt. Maybe I'm just afraid."

"Of what?"

"Everything."

"This isn't Jane Stewart I'm seein'," he said. "I may not have known you before your accident, but I do know I'm seeing a different woman."

"Brady, you've got me right where you want me. I can't even get up and walk out the door."

"What makes you think that pleases me? J.T. might like it, but not me. I want the real Dr. Jane Stewart, not this hollow imitation. Whether you walk or don't walk is secondary. I'm talking about what's going on in your head."

Tears suddenly filled her eyes. "You're right. My attitude is my problem. It has been ever since the accident."

"So what are we going to do about it?"

"I want to walk, Brady," she said. "I really do!"

"Enough to get up and do it?" He pointed toward the picnic basket sitting on the table. "Enough to walk over there with me and have lunch?"

She laughed.

"With my help," he added.

"I'll be lucky if I can stand."

"You'll have to do that first, anyway."

"Okay," she said, feeling a surge of adrenaline. "I'm going to stand up."

She unwrapped the blanket from her legs as Brady got up. Then she scooted to the edge of the bed. That much she did every day with Manuela's help. Usually, though, she slid from her bed into her chair. There was no wheelchair now—just thirty feet of empty floor to the table.

Sitting on the edge of the bed, her feet on the floor, she looked up at Brady. He had an encouraging smile on his lips and his eyes were glistening from the light of the fire. He extended one hand, which she took. Then he offered his other hand. She grasped it firmly.

"Ready?" he asked.

"I've never tried standing just holding somebody's hands."

"There's a first time for everything, sugar."

Jane swallowed hard, tightened her grip, and pulled on his hands, at the same time trying lift herself. She rose a few inches from the bed, but her legs wouldn't, couldn't, do more. They felt like jelly.

"Come on, darlin'," he said. "Push with your legs. Jump like there was a *piñata* hangin' over your head!"

She strained with all her might. Brady pulled on her hands, lifting her a bit more.

"Keep fightin'," he coaxed.

"It's no use," she said through her teeth. "I don't have any strength."

"This is the best way to get it. Don't give up."

She tried as hard as she could, but it felt like she was trying to push a piece of string. Brady lifted her a bit more. She was halfway up, breathing hard, still struggling. Moments earlier she'd been cold and wrapped in a blanket, but she felt hot now, as if tiny beads of perspiration might even have been forming on her brow.

"I can't!" she gasped.

"Yes, you can." He lifted her a bit more.

Jane was nearly erect and had nothing for support but his hands. Her body trembled and her legs shook violently, but she finally got her legs straightened and her knees locked. When she realized she'd done it, her eyes widened. "Brady, I did it!" she cried. "I stood up!"

"Damn tootin', you did it!"

He grabbed hold of her then, gathering her against him. She wrapped her arms around him. Tears bubbled from her eyes as she pressed her face to his chest, crying happily.

"You all right?" he asked. "That didn't hurt, did it?"

She shook her head, digging her fingers into the flesh of his back and inhaling his manly scent. She clung to him with all her might, and he pressed her still more firmly against him, his hand clamped tightly around her waist. When she lifted her face to him, he kissed her nose.

"You up to a stroll now?" he asked.

"I'm not sure I can even lift my foot off the floor."

"Well, let's give it a try. I'll hold my arms out from my belt and you rest your forearms on them, using them like rails. Then we'll walk over to the table."

"Just like that, huh?"

"Yeah, just like that."

First he took her by the waist with both hands as she held his shoulders. Then she slid her hands down his arms until she was standing between them, resting her forearms on his.

"Okay, let's take your first step," he said.

Jane managed to lift her foot just enough to move it a few inches. She gave a joyful little laugh.

"Terrific!" he said. "Now another."

She was able to move her other foot. Though her legs felt like the appendages on a rag doll, she was able to take a series of tiny steps. Most of her weight was on Brady's arms, but it was the closest she'd come to actually walking since the accident.

"You're doing great, Jane," he enthused.

They finally made it to the table, although the last ten feet he dragged her more than she walked. But she did feel a sense of accomplishment. Brady helped her into a chair. She looked up at him joyfully, brushing a tear from her cheek.

"Again, thanks," she said. "You're a wonderful friend."

"Darlin', I have a feelin' this is only the beginning. Truly, I do."

THE LUNCH MANUELA had packed was a gourmet meal. There was cold salmon and cheeses, croissants, crudités, a fruit salad, pastries for dessert and a bottle of Chardonnay.

They ate companionably and Jane especially enjoyed the wine. Brady leaned back in his chair as he talked about his ranch. She listened with rapt attention, her elbows on the table, her chin resting on her folded hands. She was fascinated, as much by him as by what he was saying.

"Since you don't raise cattle and haven't drilled any oil wells in a while, how do you spend your time?" she asked.

"There's a lot more to ranchin' than watching the sun rise and set," he explained, "even if you don't raise cattle. Mother Nature has a mind of her own, especially in Hill Country." Brady told her about the juniper brush that ruins rangeland by killing the grass under it. "It's a constant struggle," he said. "You let it get ahead of you and you lose what you've got."

"What do you do?"

"I hire crews to chop the cedar, which is what we call the juniper brush. It's got to be stacked and burned, and the damn stuff keeps comin' back. And it always seems like there's a washout to repair somewhere on the ranch roads."

"So you've got men working for you."

"There's Heppo, my foreman. He's Mayan Indian. Hell of a hard worker. He's got a man who works with him and most everybody else are day workers we hire. Chopping cedar occupies a lot of man-hours, but it enables me to lease my land for grazing."

"You aren't a cattleman yourself, though."

"I have several head of bison on the place."

"Not to shoot, I hope."

Brady took a big drink of wine. "No, darlin', just to admire. If you want to hunt, it'll be for deer, turkey, Russian boar, game birds and the like. There's plenty of wildlife up our way. It's rugged country, but beautiful for that reason, if no other. You'll have to come down and see for yourself."

She knew he was serious. "You mean that, don't you?"

"Damn right. Nothing would please me more."

"You know, I think I just might do that someday."

"I'd love havin' you, Jane. That's honest."

"I wouldn't be much use when it came to chopping cedar, I'm afraid. And I have no desire to shoot any animals. I guess the sunsets would have to be the main attraction."

"Do you like anthropology and history?"

"I've never studied it much," she said, "but I like museums. Why?"

"Believe it or not, my place is a veritable treasure trove of artifacts. The bottomland is covered with kitchen midden."

"What's that?"

"Sites where the early tribes set up housekeeping, leaving behind the debris of daily life. The ranch lies right across the migration route of the early peoples who inhabited the area. For centuries they crossed what is now my land, moving between their summer habitat in northern Texas and Oklahoma and their winter land in Mexico. I love digging through their mounds. It's like takin' a walk through time. Gives me a feeling of connection, of continuity with the ages."

She listened, hearing the passion in his voice. She'd never known anyone like Brady and he fascinated her.

"We get so caught up in our lives, we forget how tied to the earth we really are. An arrowhead, a few animal bones, pieces of pottery or an amulet speak volumes about what went on before we came along. Sometimes I sit at one of those long-forgotten sites, thinking how right there during centuries past babies were born, meals were prepared, old people died, battles were fought, young folks made love by the light of the moon. It's a way to look into your own heart."

She watched his shining eyes, moved. "You really are a romantic."

He smiled faintly. "I try to live with feeling . . . and passion."

"I'm glad I met you, Brady."

"No more glad than I, darlin'."

She drained the last of her wine. Brady split what was left in the bottle between them, glancing over at the fire when a log rolled off the grate. He got up and went to tend to it, adding some more wood while he was at it.

Jane watched him, admiring his lean, muscular build. All during lunch he'd been seducing her with his eyes. The subject of sex having been broached earlier, everything thereafter had been assumed—at least on Brady's part. He'd been in complete control, sending out vibrations, playing the role of conductor to her orchestra. He hadn't uttered a suggestive word, but the way he looked at her left no doubt about what he was thinking. The tension had been strong, undeniable. They both knew what was coming.

When he returned to the table, he looked at her, slowly becoming aware of the admiration on her face. "What, darlin'?" he queried.

"Will you carry me back to the bed, Brady?"

"Sure, if that's what you want."

"And will you lie down with me? I'd like for you to hold me while I listen to the rain."

He considered her soberly. "I'd have to take off these wet jeans."

Jane nodded. "I know. I want you to."

He stroked his jaw. "You aren't feelin' pressured, are you? What I mean is . . . is this what you want?"

"I'm a big girl," she replied. "My helplessness is limited to my inability to walk."

"We're changin' that, though."

She nodded.

Brady gazed at her, desire etched on his shadowed face. "You're aware that I've got a crush on you," he announced. "Sort of like love at first sight. It happened the moment you opened the door that first day."

She nodded again. "Me, too."

"You felt the same way about me?"

"Yes."

"That probably explains why we're here, then, doesn't it?"

"I guess so," she replied. "God knows, there's no other reason I'd be propositioning you."

He leaned back and chuckled, folding his arms over his chest as he continued studying her. "I'll be damned."

"You aren't going to tantalize me, are you?" she implored.

"Sweetheart, I'm savorin' the moment. I have a sneakin' suspicion it's one I'll be lookin' back on happily for a long time."

She felt a poignant desire for him, a yearning that was so strong it almost hurt. His eyes were as glossy as hers and that made the moment all the more compelling. Finally she stretched her hand across the table. Brady took it and kissed her fingers. Then, without letting go of her, he moved around the table and took her into his arms. They kissed. It was a deep, passionate kiss, and it excited her, making her heart lope and her body yearn for more.

11

THE BLAZING FIRE had warmed the room to the point where it was almost hot. Jane lay very still as Brady removed his shirt. The storm had intensified and she could hear the tattoo of the rain on the roof, a sort of low drumroll that added to the drama unfolding before her.

Brady's tall, broad-shouldered frame was muscular, well-defined. His chest was covered with a mat of dark hair, his torso tapering to a narrow waist and hips. He tossed his shirt aside and stared down at her.

Jane was acutely aware of his body. She hadn't known a man who affected her this way before, a man who made her so aware of herself. He was arousing to look at, sexual to his toes. But the effect he was having on her had another side—she felt very vulnerable; helpless to do anything but watch and wait.

"You're very beautiful," he said, before sitting on the bed beside her.

"So are you, Brady."

A slow grin crept across his face. "That's the first time anybody's ever accused me of that."

"Maybe I see you differently than others."

"Think that's it?"

She nodded.

He looked into her eyes and began molding the lines of her cheeks and jaw with his thumb. His touch sent a shiver down her spine. The more he caressed her, the more she tingled.

He didn't bother with words. This dance was physical. She studied his face, measured the vibrations coming from him. Brady had a tenderness about him, but also a latent power that engaged her sensibilities, gave her pause.

His mouth, faintly marked with a smile, was relaxed. But in his eyes she saw promise . . . and danger. Ironically, it was the danger that drew her. She lay still, waiting to see what was going to happen, wanting something to happen, wanting to feel intensely.

Brady's eyes moved over her face—testing his desires, perhaps; preparing for the next step. She had the oddest feeling that they were sharing the same longing, craving the same connection.

He drew his fingers down the side of her throat to the open vee of her shirt. When he unfastened the top button, her heart clutched. When he ran his fingers under the fabric of her shirt, her breath wedged in her throat. They looked into each other's eyes as he slowly unfastened the rest of her buttons.

Her heart was tripping. Her breathing had become shallow. Brady unfastened her bra and helped her out of it and her shirt. Exposed to the air, her nipples puckered and she shivered.

He leaned over her then, and kissed the soft undersides of her breasts, trailing his moist lips upward. Jane grew excited as he teased each nipple with his tongue. Little spasms radiated from her core. She moaned, took his head in her hands and pressed his face hard against her breast.

As he sucked and licked each bud in turn he unfastened her jeans. Jane felt a powerful well of desire.

"Oh, Brady," she groaned.

He kissed her mouth then, sensually running his tongue over the inner edges of her lips before plunging it deep into her mouth. She was breathing hard and fast, so desperately she had to turn her face away for air. He kissed her neck, washing his warm breath over her.

After holding her for several moments, Brady slipped from her arms. Before she knew what was happening, he'd pulled her jeans off her limp legs. She wore nothing but her panties. Standing over her, he followed the lines of her near-naked body with his eyes. The gesture alone made her shiver.

Without a word, Brady removed his pants and joined her on the bed, pressing the length of his body against her as they kissed again. He caressed her, running his hand over her torso, tracing her narrow waist and the curve of her hip.

Jane wanted to move her legs; she wanted to wrap them around him as she had in her dream. Instead, she used her arms to draw herself against him, to feel the hard planes of his muscular body on her soft skin. She drew her hands over his shoulders, savoring the sensation of his marblelike contours.

"You make me feel so good," she said, her face pressed against his chest. "I've never felt this way before."

A violent tremor went through her and she half bit, half kissed his skin. She pressed her face deep into the curling mat of hair, inhaling his pungent masculine scent. Another profound surge of desire flooded through her.

Brady had rolled her onto her side so that they were face-to-face. He was running his hands over her buttocks, adding to her desire. Unable to resist, she reached down and rubbed his penis through his shorts. Brady slipped his fingers under the band of her panties then, and began caressing her soft cheek.

"Darlin', I think you want me as much as I want you," he murmured.

"Oh, God, Brady," she cried. "Make love with me. Please."

He got to his knees and without hesitation pulled down her panties. Then he removed his own shorts. His sex arched gracefully from his loins.

She couldn't help staring at it, at once so threatening and inviting. She reached out and touched the velvety head. But he wouldn't let her caress him. Instead he gently pushed her legs apart and moved to the foot of the bed so that he knelt between her ankles.

Jane knew her legs had lost their firmness and tone. She only felt half a woman and it upset her. "I used to have nice legs," she murmured.

"You still do."

"No, you're just saying that."

"They need to regain their strength. And they will, sugar."

The kindness in his voice touched her. She realized then that her weakness magnified his strength.

"You aren't in pain?" he questioned. "This isn't uncomfortable?"

"Not at all. I just wish I was an equal partner."

"You're a lot more equal than you can imagine, darlin'."

The comment made her smile.

"It won't hurt you if I make love to you?" he asked softly.

Jane rolled her head back and forth on the pillow. "Not if you're gentle."

He sat back on his haunches then and caressed her feet, drawing his hands from her ankles to the tips of her toes. She liked the sensation, liked the surprising intimacy of his touch.

Next Brady ran his fingers slowly up and down her calves, making them tingle. There was more sensation in her legs than she could ever recall. They were helpless pieces of flesh, yet terribly alive in spite of their frailty. Still, she was able to wiggle her toes, make the muscles in her calves and thighs twitch.

Brady leaned forward, running his warm palms up her thighs. He drew his hands up and down her legs several times, rotating them from the outsides to the insides and back again, making her tingle. As he worked her thighs, his eyes lingered on her breasts, the mound between her legs, her face.

"Give me the other pillow," he said, after caressing her legs for several minutes.

Unsure what he had in mind, Jane handed it to him. Brady lifted her then and wedged the pillow under her hips, creating a natural curve in her lower back and at the same time opening her to him.

"Is that comfortable?" he asked.

She nodded, swallowing hard. Brady moved forward then. Above her on this hands and knees, he lowered his face to her belly, tenderly kissing her flesh.

She felt her stomach quiver as he ran his tongue around her navel. Then he dragged his lips down to her mound, skirting her fringe to the top of her leg, which he kissed. For a second she didn't breathe.

He moved farther down the bed and kissed the inside of her knee, making her leg twitch. When he started drawing his tongue up the inside of her thigh, she gasped. Brady kissed his way to the vee of her legs.

When she felt his warm breath on her she closed her eyes, giving herself up completely to the sensation.

His caresses were wonderful. She felt her juices start to flow. All her awareness was on the nerve endings at her center. Her body tensed in anticipation as his hot breath again washed over her. When at last his tongue swept over her nub, her body clenched and she cried out.

"Oh... God!"

Brady gently stroked her with his tongue, sending waves from her core. But she didn't want to come—not yet.

She reached down and took his head, lifting it from her. "Make love with me," she pleaded. "I want you in me."

He moved between her legs and gently parted them wider. Her heart was pounding, but she hardly noticed. She clenched the sheet in her fists as he wedged himself between her legs. And when she felt him at her opening, she stopped breathing entirely.

Then he entered her. He was large and hard and he filled her completely. She took him by the shoulders, tensing. Brady froze.

"Are you all right, sugar?"

"You're so big," she stammered.

"I'll be gentle."

She grew accustomed to the feel of him and her fear turned to hunger. She took his buttocks in her hands and pressed him into her more deeply, opening her legs as best she could. Brady steadily plunged into her with long smooth strokes that teased and pleasured at the same time. Jane was ready to explode. Cries of pleasure bubbled from her throat.

She erupted in a sudden cataclysm. Her body rippled beneath his, as wave after wave washed over her.

At last it was over and her body seemed to collapse. Brady was kissing her, but she hardly knew it. She was struggling for air, slowly becoming conscious of the magnitude of what had happened.

"Oh, my God," she said, panting. "That was incredible."

"Are you all right?" he whispered into her ear.

"I've never . . . felt so good in my life."

He kissed her neck.

"I feel like I could float right out of here," she said. "I don't need to walk."

He laughed, easing himself out of her. Dropping beside her, he rolled her toward him and looked into her eyes. Jane stared at him with awe. Lover, stranger, phantom, mystery man, friend—he was all those things. And the reality of what had just happened was almost impossible to grasp.

"I love you, Jane," he said, his eyes shimmering.

She touched his brow.

"That's awfully quick, I know," he added, "but it's the way I feel, and I've never been one to let politics, manners or good taste get in the way of a truthful word."

"It's the way I feel, too," she told him. "So I understand. And I guess there's no harm in saying it."

Jane sighed, feeling deep contentment. She listened to the rain. It was coming down heavier than ever. The smell of sex was all about them and her body was still faintly throbbing.

Brady held her close. She absently stroked his shoulder, liking the warmth of his skin. "That was very special," she said. "Maybe not for you, but it was for me."

"Now why would you think it wasn't special for me?"

"I could tell you've done that before. You're no amateur when it comes to satisfying a woman, Mr. Coleman."

"What are you saying?"

"I've never experienced anything quite like that," she said with a laugh. "Believe me."

"It was special for me, too. Very special. I've never felt quite the same way before." Brady stroked her hair but he was silent, as if he was trying to find the right words. "It's the first time it was more than just sex," he finally said.

Jane wasn't sure exactly what he was trying to say. When it occurred to her he might really be serious about feeling love for her, it gave her pause.

"Love and sex are a new combination for me," he said after a moment, confirming her thoughts.

"Don't make the mistake of confusing love and compassion, Brady."

He didn't reply. But he did roll onto his back and stare at the flickering shadows on the ceiling. Free of his embrace, she became aware of the coolness of the air and shivered. He reached down and pulled the covers up over them. For a while they lay in silence.

"I don't mean to diminish what happened," she finally said. "It was the most wonderful sexual experience of my life. But we have to keep it in perspective."

Brady still didn't respond.

"Are you upset with me?" she asked, after waiting a minute or two for him to speak.

"No, darlin', how could I be?"

"You're being so quiet. What are you thinking?"

"I was thinking we should spend the night here."

"At the cottage?"

"Yep."

"Why?"

"Just to make sure it wasn't a fluke."

She laughed. "Manuela is expecting me home."

"Why don't you call her on my cellular phone and tell her you've had a better offer?"

She put her hand on his chest, then pressed her face into it, filling her nostrils with his scent. Recollections of what he'd done to her went tumbling pleasantly through her mind. She cuddled close to him. "I suppose I could."

"I wouldn't want to twist your arm, darlin'."

"Brady, you know there's not a woman on earth who can resist you."

"But you're the only one I care about."

It was surprising how badly she wanted to believe that. Even knowing that she shouldn't, she did. She ran her hand over the level plane of his stomach and down to his loins. His penis was soft, but still large. Under her touch, it began coming to life. She released it, stroking his legs instead.

"What do you say, sugar?"

"All right, Brady," she said, kissing his chest. "I'll call Manuela."

He got the cellular phone. Jane telephoned her housekeeper, saying they'd decided to stay at the cottage rather than try to brave the storm. Jane suspected Manuela was pleased by the news. She liked Brady, and it was no wonder that she did. He was very likable. Seductive.

They dozed in each other's arms for a couple of hours after that. The intensity of the storm abated, but it continued to rain. Whenever she awoke she would listen to the elements, or the crackling fire. Sometimes the wind would kick up and blow the rain hard against the windows. One such gust awakened her abruptly and she lifted her head to look outside, seeing that darkness was falling.

Brady continued to sleep beside her, as peaceful and contented as a lamb. Jane watched him, seeing him as her lover and realizing the thought pleased her. Time having passed and a sense of reality having sunk in, she should have been shocked about the way she felt, but she wasn't. Even though she hardly knew the man, she felt very comfortable with him. He had the capacity for putting a person at ease, probably because he was so open and straightforward. And he made her feel good about herself.

Inevitably, though, she began asking herself where it would lead. The answer came with surprising ease. No place. This interlude with Brady Coleman was just that—an interlude. One of those unique experiences a woman can have, if she's lucky—a sexy dream come to life. Brady was her fantasy man, her Texas cowboy. She'd carry him and this rainy afternoon in her heart forever, a secret memory to look back on fondly through marriage and family and whatever else came into her life.

Wonderful as the experience had been, it was meant for today alone. That was plain. She would be a fool to think otherwise. And Jane Stewart was no fool.

12

MORNING BROUGHT a brief respite from the storm. It had stopped raining when Jane awoke, but the skies were gray and more trouble seemed to be brewing off the coast. Brady already had a fire going by the time she propped her head up on a pillow and said good-morning.

"How's my angel?" he asked, coming over to the bed.

Jane had pulled the covers up under her chin. She smiled, dreading the thought of how she must look. Brady, of course, had a day's growth of beard, but it added to his rugged, masculine image.

"An angel, I'm not," she said.

He sat down beside her, tweaking her chin. "Angels are entitled to their fun, same as anybody else, darlin'."

Jane blushed deeply, which was obviously what he intended. He was alluding to their night of lovemaking. From dark until midnight they'd made love. She'd never thought of herself as having a particularly ravenous appetite for sex, but that was before Brady Coleman. He was a lover par excellence, an expert on the female body, a master. He'd shown her erogenous zones she didn't know she had. Above all, he made her feel cherished and whole, loved as she'd never been loved before.

"If I'm an angel," she said, "I'm a fallen one."

"Why do you say that?"

"Because I spent the night with a devil!"

Brady laughed his robust, good-natured laugh. "You've been deprived, sugar, that's all."

Jane held his hand and smiled into his eyes. "You're a wonderful lover," she said with genuine admiration. "You really are."

"And you're a sweetheart to say so. I must say, though, I had wonderful inspiration. I've never felt about anyone the way I feel about you, Jane. Last night was very special."

She rubbed the back of his hand affectionately. "Well, you made me feel very, very good. And I don't just mean physically."

He leaned over and kissed her. "I don't know about you, Doc," he said, "but I could use a Texas-size breakfast about now. Snacking on leftovers for dinner is one thing, but a man's got to have his breakfast and there's not a thing in the house."

"I can get dressed and we can go," she said.

"It occurred to me I could run down to that little store we passed up the highway a piece and pick up something. I don't cook well, but I cook hearty."

"You're really a lot more paternal than you realize, Brady."

That made him grin. "You come back to Texas with me, darlin', get a few weeks of exercise and some good ranch cookin', and I'll have you dancin' the jig inside two weeks."

"It's a tempting offer," she said, meaning it, "but I think we should worry about breakfast first."

"Hungry?"

"Yes, but what I'd really give my eyeteeth for is a nice hot bath."

"There's good news in that department, too," he said. "I checked the hot-water heater. It had been turned off. That was the only problem."

"You mean there's hot water?"

"All your little heart desires. I'd have taken a shower myself, but I wanted to give the tank a chance to heat up. If you like, you can have your bath while I run down to the store, and I can grab a shower after breakfast."

"Sounds delicious," she said.

Brady had gotten her wheelchair from the car so that she could get around the cottage on her own. He'd also found an old terry bathrobe in a closet, which he brought and helped her into. When she was ready to go to the bath, Brady asked if she felt like trying to walk.

"You're determined to get me on my feet, aren't you?"

"Like the man said, you can't dance until you walk."

Brady was standing, his hands on his hips. Jane looked up at him. "You know, it's possible I may never be able to do much more than hobble around," she said. "The jury's still out on the extent of my recovery."

"We'll just have to play the hand we're dealt, darlin'. I don't see any other choice. As my mama used to say, there's no point in frettin' over things you can't change."

The use of "we" in reference to the future did not go unnoticed, but Jane saw no point in commenting on it. Somehow she wasn't surprised. She believed that he truly regarded their relationship as extraordinary; she just didn't know why. Before they'd fallen asleep he'd told her again that he loved her. She hadn't told him so, but she knew people couldn't fall in love in the course of a couple of days. Nor had she expressed her misgivings about what motivated him.

Between sessions of lovemaking they'd talked a lot. In a roundabout way Brady had discussed his feelings toward her as well as his intentions. "My daddy used to say a man's feelings about a thing should be treated like a good horse. You ride 'em until either you or it gives out. Life has a way of letting you know when a thing's over."

Brady Coleman's homespun wisdom was a part of his colorful personality and it added to her fascination with him. But she wasn't sure how seriously to take him. And she was even more uncertain how seriously to consider her own feelings for him. More than once she'd caught herself wondering if it was possible he might turn out to be more than just the interlude she'd thought him to be.

"So what'll it be?" Brady asked. "Walk or ride?"

"I'll try to walk," she said.

"Thatta girl!" He beamed.

Jane scooted to the edge of the bed and swung her legs over the side. Brady stood in front of her, offering his hands. She gripped them firmly.

"Do as much lifting as you can with your legs," he instructed. "I'll help only as much as necessary."

She took a deep breath and set her jaw, knowing it would be a challenge. "All right," she said, "here goes."

She leaned forward and strained as hard as she could to get to her feet. At first she was barely able to lessen her weight on the mattress, but when Brady lifted her, she got her momentum going. Eventually she rose to her feet. As before, her legs were wobbly, but she wasn't as unsteady as she'd been in the past. That made her happy.

"Much better!" he enthused. "We'll be waltzin' by the end of the week."

Jane couldn't help a girlish laugh. It was a small feat, but it excited her. Brady looked as happy as she did. Happiness, gratitude, love and a whole bevy of other emotions flooded her heart. She spontaneously threw her arms around his neck.

"Thank you, Brady. Thank you so much."

He held her. "There's nothin' to thank me for, darlin'. You're the one who stood up."

She pressed her head against his. "You'll never know."

With a lot of help, she managed to drag herself to the bathroom. Brady ran the water in the tub for her and brought in her wheelchair. She'd soak while he went to the store. With the wheelchair nearby, she felt reasonably secure. On a couple of occasions she'd gotten in and out of the tub without help, so she was confident she'd be all right. But she did let him help her into the tub before he left.

Brady gave her a kiss goodbye and Jane eased down into the water. It felt heavenly. The bathroom window was open a crack at the top and, in the stillness of the cottage, she was able to hear the rain, which had started again. Moments later she heard Brady's car start, and then she heard him drive off.

Alone, Jane felt a glow of contentment. This whole thing was crazy, but Brady had made her very happy and that couldn't be ignored. It might only be a passing fancy, but she was enjoying it. And she liked him very, very much. It was a heady feeling. Almost like being in love.

For the next ten or fifteen minutes she soaked in the tub and mused. Mostly she thought about Brady and the past twenty-four hours. If the water hadn't started getting tepid she might have been able to lie there all day. It was a bit of a drive to the store, so it would be some time before he'd be back.

She'd begun thinking about climbing out of the tub when she heard his car. He'd made the trip faster than she'd anticipated. Or had she lost track of time? Maybe it had been longer than she realized.

Rather than rush to get out, she decided to wait for him. The chances of slipping and taking a header were considerable, and there was no point in taking an unnecessary risk.

The rain picked up in intensity. She listened to it blow against the cottage. Poor Brady. He'd be soaked. Maybe this time she'd be able to get him to take off his pants and dry them by the fire. They were beyond modesty.

She heard what sounded like rapping at the front door and wondered why he would knock. Even with his arms full of groceries, he knew she couldn't easily come to help him. But then she heard the door open and figured he was probably trying to push it with his foot or something. The door closed and Jane cocked her ear, listening.

"Brady?" she called. When there was no response, she called out again. "Brady? Is that you?"

Still no response. Then she heard footsteps. An eerie feeling came over her, a sense that something was wrong.

"Brady?"

Just then Jeremy appeared in the doorway. She gasped, crossing her arms over her breasts.

"Wrong lover," he said dourly. "Surprise."

"Jeremy," she muttered with horror. "What are you doing here?"

"The better question is, what are *you* doing here?" He gave a sadistic laugh. "But maybe that's obvious," he said bitterly. "Where is he, anyway?"

Jane stared at him, mute. She was outraged, but too shocked to sputter the necessary words of rebuke.

Jeremy was in a trench coat, the front and shoulders of which were soaked. His face and hair were wet, too, and he looked angry—so angry it frightened her.

"Where is he?" he barked again.

"He went to the store," she stammered.

He glanced at the wheelchair next to the tub and the robe draped over it. "I suppose he drew your bath before he left."

"Jeremy, I resent you barging in this way. You have no—"

"And by the look of things he's rendered a few other services, as well," he accused, interrupting her. "Or was it you who rendered the service, Jane? Brady Coleman's had all the whores in Texas. He might as well try his luck in California. And why not start at the top?"

"You bastard!" she shouted. "Get out of here!"

He chuckled, though he looked more sinister and crazed than amused. "The indignation doesn't ring true, Jane, dear. You've been exposed for what you really are."

"I'm warning you, Jeremy," she said through her teeth. "Leave this house immediately! Go!"

He threw back his head and laughed.

"What's the matter with you?" she cried. "What do you want? What do you hope to gain?"

His expression hardened. "What do I hope to gain? I think we're beyond that," he retorted, flushing. "It's what I've lost!"

She glared, feeling terribly vulnerable. He was up to no good, but she didn't know what. Her heart was pounding and the water was cold. She began shivering.

"If you're referring to me, I was never yours, Jeremy," she said, trying to sound calm and reasonable.

He moved from the doorway into the bathroom. "Oh, you were mine, all right," he said, his eyes widening as he sat down in her wheelchair. "Mine until that bastard Coleman came along."

He reached over and casually touched her face, slowly dragging his index finger across her cheekbone. Jane recoiled.

"Brady is a decent, caring human being," she said.

Jeremy sneered. "Brady Coleman isn't worthy of cleaning my shoes. And you're no better."

Jane flushed. If she were able, she'd have jumped out of the tub and pummeled him. But she was in no position to attack anyone. To the contrary, she was probably in danger and needed to get rid of this maniac any way she could. Her mind started spinning. Where was Brady and how long would it be before he returned?

"Your feelings toward me are clear," she said as calmly as she was able. "You've said what you have to say, so why don't you leave?"

"Because I'm enjoying this."

He ran his hand down the side of her throat, nonchalantly wrapping his fingers around her neck. Jane grabbed his wrist and pushed his hand away.

Jeremy smirked. "Anyway, I've got unfinished business. I've decided to settle things with Brady once and for all."

He was staring at her body. Trembling, Jane folded her arms across her breasts. She'd never felt so exposed and unprotected in her life. It was like a horrible dream.

"I'm sure he'll accommodate you," she said bravely. "But meanwhile you have no reason to torment me. Why don't you wait in the other room?"

"Because I want to wait here," he said, his eyes moving over her.

He dropped his arm over the side of the tub and let his fingers dangle in the water. His expression was diabolical. God only knew what he intended.

"That night I slept with you, I could have had you," he said, almost sounding miffed. "You were mine for the asking."

She hardened her glare. Though she was afraid, she lashed back. "You're showing your true colors. All you're doing is proving to me that I was right to reject you!"

"You didn't reject me!" he roared. "Nobody rejects me!" He jumped to his feet, his face bright red. "*I'm* the one who rejects. You were mine and so was your money." Jeremy started pacing. "That money was mine. I earned it. She wanted me to have it because she loved me! Lies, lies. All he told was lies!"

Jane stared. He wasn't making any sense. Was he crazy? Had he flipped out?

"What are you looking at?" he shouted.

"This is all about money, isn't it?"

"They're trying to take away what's mine. All of them! Especially that bastard, Coleman."

"Jeremy, you need help."

His eyes widened in a deranged-looking way. "Help? Why? I took care of Leigh, didn't I? And Victoria, too! The were both whores." He began pacing more quickly, looking agitated.

He'd completely lost control. Suddenly the stories of what had happened to his wives seemed entirely credible. Jeremy, it appeared, was indeed a Dr. Jekyll/Mr. Hyde.

"You wanted me," he said, shaking his head. "You were in love with me and you'd have married me. But you didn't give me a chance. You tried to take away what I'd worked so hard for. Wasn't I kind to you? Didn't I sacrifice?"

"All you wanted was my money, Jeremy," she said, as much to herself as to him.

"But you wanted me!"

She began shaking violently. "I never loved you. I don't want you near me. I'm getting cold. I've got to get out of the tub. Please, go into the other room, if you insist on waiting for Brady. I'm very uncomfortable."

"Well, I'll take care of that," he replied with a horrible laugh.

Reaching down, he grabbed the stopper chain and yanked it hard. The water began draining away. Jeremy stood there, his hands on his hips, watching her body emerge from the receding water, a deranged smile on his lips.

"No!" she cried, her hand and arm still placed over her private parts. "Don't do this. Please!"

Jeremy seemed not to hear her pleas. Tears filled her eyes and she began to cry. She looked up at him through her tears, seeing the man Brady had warned her about, the demon who hid behind a charming veneer.

His grin suddenly broke at the sound of a vehicle down at the drive. He cocked his head. They realized at the same moment that Brady had returned.

"Now maybe you'll leave," she sobbed.

Jeremy glared down at her. "For now, my darling," he said, reaching under his coat. "But I'll be back later to finish this little chat."

As he turned, Jane saw the flash of a metal object in his hand. It was a gun.

BRADY'S BLOOD RAN COLD the second he saw the Legend parked in the drive. He pulled his car right up against the rear bumper of the vehicle and jumped out.

Leaving the groceries in the car, he began running up the path, intuitively petrified at what he might find. If the bastard had so much as laid a hand on her, he'd kill him—kill him with his bare hands.

The path was slippery. Brady fell twice, but he quickly scrambled to his feet. He arrived at the cottage breathless and dashed up the stairs. Throwing the door wide open, he saw J.T. standing in front of the fireplace, his hands in the pockets of his trench coat, a stupid grin on his face.

"Where is she?" Brady demanded, his chest heaving.

"Who?"

"Jane, you sonovabitch. What have you done with her?"

"When last I saw her, she was bathing." He smiled. "A delightful sight, believe me."

Brady started toward the bathroom, but Trent pulled his hand from his pocket, revealing a nickel-plated automatic.

"Hold it," he said.

Brady stopped in his tracks.

"I think the lady prefers privacy. But if not, I'll look in on her once you and I have finished our conversation."

Brady ignored the smirk on J.T.'s face. "Jane," he called out loudly, "are you all right?"

"Yes" came a voice from the back of the house. "I'm okay. But be careful. Jeremy has a gun."

"He's already made that discovery, my dear," Jeremy shouted back.

"Look, Trent," Brady snapped, "what do you want?"

"What do I want? What do I want?" Jeremy roared. "I want you off my back! To quit stealing what's mine! Everything was fine till you came along. Wasn't Leigh's ranch enough for you? Why did you have to come after Jane, too? Didn't you know I'd had it up to here with you?" he snarled, drawing the barrel of the gun across his throat.

"You're a murderer and a thief," Brady retorted. "This proves it."

"Ha! What do *you* know? You know nothing, Coleman. You're an ignorant cowboy."

"Maybe so, J.T., but I know you killed my sister. And you tried to kill that other woman in Connecticut."

Jeremy began laughing. "Kill? Why should I kill them? They loved me. Both of them."

"Then why did you squeeze the life out of Leigh? Because you loved her?"

J.T.'s expression turned hard. "She didn't understand. She didn't understand."

"You got that right. She didn't understand what a slimeball you are."

J.T.'s jaw clenched. "She got just what she deserved. I couldn't help it if she wouldn't understand!" He began waving the gun wildly. "I'm glad she's dead. Glad!"

Rage welled up in Brady. He pulled off his sheepskin coat and tossed it aside. Then he took a step toward J.T., stopping only when the barrel of the gun was leveled on his chest.

"So did you strangle Leigh before or after you shot Spike Adamson?" he demanded.

Jeremy threw back his head and laughed.

"Is that the gun you shot him with, J.T.?"

"I had to," Jeremy said flatly. "I had no choice."

"So you killed Leigh first, then you went and got a street bum to break in so you could shoot him. What did you promise him, J.T.? Was it money or your wife?"

"Aren't you the smug one," Trent sneered. "Too stupid to see I did you a favor. You'll have that ranch in a few years, so what's the problem?"

"You lowlife," Brady said through his teeth.

"Why couldn't you leave well enough alone?" J.T. went on. "Why didn't you stay in Texas? What good to you is a woman in a wheelchair, anyway? It couldn't be for the sex. It had to be because of me. You couldn't stand seeing me get my due."

Brady shook his head with contempt.

"It doesn't matter," J.T. said. "You aren't going to get in my hair again. I'm going to make sure of that." He pointed the automatic.

"You know, J.T., I'm surprised you had the guts to come here. Creeps like you are gutless. You'd rather strangle a woman in her bed than face a real enemy."

Jeremy threw back his head and laughed. "You don't understand, either," he said. "You're fools. All of you!"

"Well, I understand this much. You're going to pay for what you've done." Slowly, Brady started moving toward him. "Even if it means breaking your neck with my bare hands."

Jeremy extended the gun toward Brady's chest. "You're making it easy for me, big brother."

Brady froze, realizing J.T. was crazy enough to pull the trigger. He seethed, contemplating his next move. Four feet separated them. The question was if he could wrest the gun away before Jeremy got off a shot.

"Well, I didn't come here to talk," J.T. said. "So, adios, cowboy. It's been nice knowing you."

"No, Jeremy, don't!" Jane screamed.

Brady and J.T. whipped their heads toward her simultaneously. Jane was sitting in her chair at the door, wearing the old terry bathrobe. The distraction was the opportunity Brady needed.

He lunged for J.T., knocking the gun from his hand. But, in the process it went off, the round catching Brady in the shoulder and spinning him around. As he fell, he heard Jane scream and saw the weapon go skidding across the floor and into the fire.

Jeremy scrambled to the fireplace and tried to snatch the gun from the coals, but the heat was too intense. When he saw Brady stagger to his feet, he bolted for the door, pushing Brady down again as he shoved past him.

Brady got back up as J.T. went out the front door. It was then that he became aware of the searing pain in his shoulder. A stream of blood flowed down his arm. His palm was bloody. A red puddle was forming on the floor at his feet. Jane wheeled toward him.

"You've been hurt!" she exclaimed, terrified.

"It's just my shoulder."

"Let me see. I need to look at it."

But Brady couldn't wait. "I've got to stop J.T.," he said, heading for the door.

"No, Brady!" Jane called after him. "You can't go out there, you're bleeding too heavily!"

He was too concerned about J.T. to heed her warning. At the door he was able to see that Jeremy was already halfway down the path to the drive. But he wouldn't be going anywhere in his car; Brady had pinned the Legend in by parking right behind it.

He glanced back at Jane, who had a stricken expression on her face. "Use my cellular phone to call the sheriff," he instructed. Grabbing his shoulder, he hurried out the door and into the rain, intent on one thing and one thing only—catching his sister's killer.

13

JANE WAS IN A NEAR PANIC, but she did what Brady told her—she phoned the sheriff's office and described what had happened. They promised to dispatch a car as well as an ambulance.

After making the call she wheeled to the front door. From there she was able to see the path leading down to the drive. To her surprise, Brady and Jeremy were both on it, trudging back up toward the cottage. Brady had hold of Jeremy's arm. They were both covered with mud. It appeared they'd struggled and Brady had won.

The rain was coming down in a torrent. The two men slogged along heavily, looking exhausted. When they were about halfway to the cottage, Brady stopped. He appeared winded, and Jane figured he was further weakened from his loss of blood.

Jeremy must have been aware of Brady's distress because he suddenly jerked his arm free and headed back down the slope, toward the ocean. Brady turned and staggered after him.

Jane forced her way onto the porch. "Brady!" she cried. "Let him go! It doesn't matter. You're hurt!"

But if Brady heard, he didn't heed her plea. A chill went down her spine. The path Jeremy had taken led to the promontory overlooking the sea cliff. There was no way down the face of it. He'd be trapped. And once

Brady had him cornered, there'd be another fight. She was sure of it.

Her breath wedged in her throat, Jane saw Jeremy arrive at the promontory. He peered over the edge. It was probably then that he realized he was trapped. She imagined the terror he must have felt. It was a dangerous place. Her parents had forbidden her and Margaret to go near the cliff when they were children.

But it wasn't Jeremy she was concerned about. It was Brady, wounded and bleeding, yet determined to track down his sister's killer. Knowing how dangerous the cliff was, she was absolutely petrified. All she could do, though, was watch the drama unfold.

BRADY STAGGERED forward. His head was spinning and his vision was blurred. He had to stop every few steps to rest. The pain in his shoulder was excruciating—even worse than when he'd dislocated it playing football.

Ahead of him, at the tip the promontory, J.T. turned to face him, his eyes wide with fear. But he also had that crazed look of a man completely out of touch with reality. Like a caged animal.

Brady took a step forward, trying to disguise how weak he felt. He had to be ready for anything. If Jeremy tried to dash past him, there'd be no room for the bastard to maneuver. Brady was glad about that, though. He'd waited years for this. Now he had his little sister's killer in his sights. J.T. was exactly where he wanted him.

Brady moved closer, taking perverse pleasure from the look of terror on Jeremy's face. They were ten or fifteen feet apart. The rain pounded down. They were both soaked. He knew this was going to be it—a fight to the death.

"It's payback time," Brady said through his teeth. "This is for Leigh. For the life you snatched away, you filthy murderer."

Jeremy shook his head, but he didn't say anything. Brady inched closer. His wounded arm was weak. He couldn't lift it but he clenched his fist anyway, holding it at his waist like an arm-weary prizefighter.

When only a couple of feet separated them, Jeremy started making strange whimpering sounds. His head made jerky movements as he seemed to be scanning the ground for something. Then he bent over and picked up a rock. Brady knew then that he'd been searching for a weapon. He rushed forward, throwing his good shoulder into J.T.'s chest, hoping to knock him off-balance before he could throw the rock.

The force of the charge carried them both backward, but somehow they kept their footing. J.T. clung to him for dear life, making it impossible for Brady to pull back far enough to get in a punch with his good arm.

Jeremy raised the stone over his head. Brady saw the blow coming, but before he could ward it off, the rock crashed onto his skull and everything went black.

JANE WATCHED WITH HORROR as Brady slumped to the ground. But on his way down he hit Jeremy's legs with enough force that his feet slid out from under him and he began slipping backward.

It took only a moment, but to Jane it seemed like an attenuated sequence played out in slow motion—each fraction of a second a separate snapshot. As she watched, Jeremy clawed at the muddy earth, but he couldn't stop the momentum of his slide. He went over the edge of the cliff and out of sight.

Suddenly all was still down at the cliff. Brady's motionless body lay like the carcass of a dead animal. Tears streaked down Jane's face as she prayed that he'd move, lift his head—anything to show he was alive. But he just lay there, some forty or fifty yards away. Was he dead?

At best, his life was in danger. He'd been bleeding heavily and could die from loss of blood, if not from shock and exposure. How long before an ambulance arrived? And where was the sheriff? Big Sur was remote, and the cottage more so. It could be fifteen or twenty minutes before anyone got there—perhaps more, given the weather.

Jane knew she had to do something. But she couldn't walk and there was no way she could maneuver her wheelchair down the steep slope. That left one alternative: she'd crawl. If the ambulance arrived in the meantime, so much the better.

But she needed to be prepared in case she got to Brady first. She'd have to stop the bleeding. For that she needed cloth for a compress. And for shock, she needed a blanket to cover him and preserve his body heat.

She wheeled back into the house, got some cloths from the kitchen, a blanket off the bed and Brady's phone. Then she returned to the porch. Looking down at the promontory, she saw that nothing had changed. She bundled everything in the blanket and, slipping from her chair, began bumping her way on her bottom down the steps, using her hands and dragging her legs.

Thankfully the tall, wet grass was more forgiving than the wooden steps. She was able to use her hands and elbows to pull herself along on her stomach. The rain soaked her within minutes. The robe was like a wet blanket.

She had scarcely gone fifteen yards before she was exhausted. She'd been cut and scraped by the vegetation. If only she could crawl properly. But her legs were useless. Then she remembered how she and her sister had rolled down the slope as kids. Letting gravity do the work was a way to move faster. But she had to make sure she could do it and still keep hold of the blanket.

Turning at right angles to the direction of the slope, she let herself roll down the steepest part, coming to a stop within ten yards of the promontory. She'd lost the tie to her robe, making it impossible to keep it closed, but she was able to see Brady and didn't have much farther to go.

He hadn't moved, which wasn't a good sign. He was either unconscious or dead. Jane dragged herself over the last section of gritty, muddy ground, scraping her stomach and thighs in the process.

By the time she got to Brady's side, her elbows were a bloody mess. She was badly chilled, but thrilled to find him still breathing. She covered him with the blanket, checked the dilation of his pupils, then pressed her finger to his carotid artery. His pulse was much weaker than she'd have liked, but he didn't appear to be in immediate danger. There was a nasty lump on the side of his head and some bleeding from his scalp. A concussion was likely.

Next she examined the bullet wound. The entire side of his shirt and one sleeve were soaked with blood. He'd lost a pint or two, maybe more. She took the cloths she'd brought and made a compress to stem the bleeding.

There wasn't anything more she could do except pray. Her adrenaline had kept her going, but the cold was catching up with her. She got under the blanket, reasoning that sharing body heat would benefit them both.

The next priority was to alert the emergency crew to where they were. Fortunately the phone wasn't damaged. She got the dispatcher and updated her on Brady's condition. She was told the responding units were five minutes away at most.

Jane was trembling violently, but she at least had hope. Putting the phone aside, she hugged Brady and put additional pressure on his wound.

"Help's on the way," she whispered into his ear. "Hang on, honey. I don't want to lose you." She pressed her face to his icy cheek and stared up at the sky.

After a while she could hear a siren in the distance. It came from down on the coast highway most probably. Thank God, she thought. It wouldn't be long now.

Listening intently, she could hear the surf pounding on the rocks. There was also the tattoo of the falling rain. Then she heard something else. A groan. She lifted her head to look at Brady, but he was still unconscious.

She heard the sound again. It was coming from the cliff!

Brady mumbled just then, and she turned her attention to him.

"Oh . . . God," he murmured. "My head."

Her heart soared. "It's all right, darling, I'm here," she said, kissing his cheek. "Help's on the way. It'll be just a few minutes."

Brady's eyelids fluttered. He lifted his head.

"Just rest," she said. "Don't try to move."

But then his dazed expression turned to horror. At that instant Jane saw something from the corner of her eye—a head and shoulders rising over the edge of the cliff. It was Jeremy, his face smeared with mud and blood, his eyes wide and crazed.

Jane froze. It was as though he'd risen from the dead. He hadn't slid far, probably only to the ledge below.

"You won't get me," he muttered, obviously out of his mind. "I'll kill you both."

She watched as he crawled slowly toward them. "Stay there, Jeremy," she pleaded. "Help is coming. They'll take you to the hospital, too. Don't come any closer. You're hurt. You need help."

But he ignored her pleading. He inched forward, digging his fingers into the mud.

"You've got...to stop him, Jane," Brady groaned, his chest heaving. "He's...nuts."

Jeremy kept coming, inch by inch, his eyes locked on hers. He was almost at her feet and showed no intention of stopping.

"I'll get you both," he muttered over the sound of the raging storm.

"Get away!" she screamed at him. "The police are coming!"

He was making his way alongside her legs now.

"Jeremy, don't! Please!"

He paused, but only to pick up another rock. It was the size of a cantaloupe and he had to struggle to get it over his head. He was on his knees, ready to crash the rock down on them. He'd kill them, crush their skulls. Brady was helpless. She was their only chance.

Throwing the flap of the blanket off her, Jane lifted her leg, and with difficulty planted it in the middle of his chest. Then, using the last ounce of her energy, she pushed with all her might. She scarcely managed to move him, but it was enough to throw him off-balance. The weight of the rock carried him backward and he toppled over. He tried to right himself, but before he could, he started sliding toward the precipice. There was a look of horrified disbelief on his face, an image she'd never forget.

The last thing she saw was his shoes disappearing over the edge of the cliff. Then nothing. No scream. No cry for help. The only sounds were the crashing of the waves, the patter of the rain, and a siren coming up the drive.

JANE LAY SHIVERING in the back of the ambulance, although she was wrapped in blankets. The siren wailed as the vehicle snaked its way back up the coast toward Monterey, throwing them from side to side as it negotiated the sharp bends in the highway.

The paramedics had worked on Brady from the moment they'd arrived at the cliff. They'd given him fluids intravenously and had worked to stem the bleeding. Jane had listened and watched as best she could, but she hadn't wanted to interfere, knowing every second counted. She'd heard no sound from Brady.

Finally, she couldn't hold her tongue any longer. "How's he doing?" she asked.

"I think we got to him just in time," the paramedic said without looking back at her.

"You've got him stabilized?"

"He's in shock, but stabilizing."

The paramedic moved out of the way, enabling Jane to see Brady for the first time. She reached across the narrow aisle and took his hand. He slowly rolled his head toward her and, seeing her, smiled.

"How do you feel?" she asked.

Brady licked his lips to try to speak. "Like...I've been on...the wrong end of a stampede."

"We'll be at the hospital soon and you'll be fine."

He gave her a faint smile. "I guess . . . I owe you one, don't I, Jane?"

"I owe *you*. I hate to think what would have happened if you hadn't decided to save me—whether I wanted you to or not. I don't know how I'll ever thank you."

Brady weakly squeezed her hand. "Looks to me like you've got two choices, sugar." He took a few breaths. "You either tip your hat and say thanks and adios . . . or you come back with me to God's country."

Jane raised her brows. "It's either one or the other, huh?"

"When you come right down to it, darlin'." He coughed and took a measured breath or two. "'Course, if it's me you take...then we can go through whatever face-saving motions you want."

"Well, glad to hear you're capable of being reasonable."

He managed a sly smile. "You got a better idea?"

"I see different choices, Brady. You can either get on your horse and ride off into the sunset, or you can learn to play golf at Pebble Beach."

He considered that. "I see now we're facin' a long, difficult negotiation."

"The best things don't come easily," she said.

Brady put his hand on his bloody shoulder. "Sugar, you aren't tellin' me anything I don't already know, believe me."

She smiled pleasantly.

He drew a long breath. "It's only fair to warn you, darlin'. I've got one thing goin' for me you'll be hard-pressed to overcome."

"And what's that, pray tell?"

"You ain't never seen a Hill Country sunset."

Epilogue

BRADY STEPPED OUT onto the back porch at dawn.
Large white flakes of snow were drifting down like tiny
parachutes from the leaden sky. He turned his face to
the heavens to let the moist flakes plop onto his skin.
They were like soft kisses from an angel. Maybe it was
Leigh, he thought, liking the notion.

He was still warm from his bed, but the biting air
nipped at his ears and nose. He turned up the fleece
collar of his coat, pulled his hat down over his brow,
and began walking toward the barn, his hands stuffed
in his pockets.

Brady thought the snow-dusted landscape looked
like a fairyland, and so very different from the Texas of
his memory. Snow was certainly not unheard of in the
Hill Country—once or twice each winter a storm from
the plains would make its way that far south, but usually it came howling down the canyons. This was a
gentle dusting, a brushstroke from Nature's palate, and
it was pretty as could be.

He scanned the landscape beyond the barn, barely
able to make out the frost-glazed rim of the canyon
walls. There was an inch of snow on the ground. Considering how late it was in the season it would likely be

gone by early afternoon, so if he was going to show it to Scotty, they couldn't wait long after breakfast.

Brady smiled at the thought. This would be the baby's first close-up look at snow. He remembered well his own first time, although of course he'd been a bit older—probably three or four. Snow was rare in San Antonio, but they had gotten a few inches one winter day long ago.

Brady remembered his mother bundling him up and his father taking him into the backyard to make a snowman. They had rolled and rolled, using every square inch of the lawn, finally managing to make a couple of balls the size of watermelons. Brady recalled stacking them up, adding sticks for arms and his softball for a head. His mother had drawn a face with a stick and topped it with a stocking for a hat. By the next morning nothing was left of the snowman but the softball, but the memory had always stayed with him.

That softball snowman had been his first, last and only one. He wondered if at eighteen months Scotty would be too young to appreciate this ritual of childhood. Even if he was, Brady would have this memory to go with his own. Yes, he'd ask Jane to bundle up Scotty after breakfast and he'd take him out in the yard to play in the snow.

Brady came to the barn, pulled open the heavy door and went inside. The mare was stamping nervously in her stall, a pretty good indication she hadn't yet dropped her foal. He went to the gate of the stall.

"Still no baby, huh, girl?" he said to the horse.

The mare tossed her head and stamped her foot. Normally she'd have come to him, but evidently she wanted no part of anyone.

"You're not the only one who's anxious," he said soothingly. "I promised Jane we'd head for California as soon as you have Junior, so if you don't get with it soon, my life's goin' to turn pretty miserable."

The mare finally came to him, tossing her head when he reached out to stroke her nose. Brady chuckled.

"I guess I don't have to tell you, females can get kinda testy when they're impatient over somethin'." He reached down and took a handful of oats from a bucket on the floor and gave it to the mare. She chomped it up and stamped off, swishing her tail at him as she turned away. "Guess I won't be gettin' any sympathy here," he chided. "Holler, if you need anything, old girl. I'm goin' back to bed."

Brady left the barn, making the long walk back to the house. Leigh was still sending down her snow kisses and he gratefully accepted a few, his face upturned to the sky.

"I love you, darlin'," he said, smiling heavenward. "Damn, if I don't wish you could meet my family."

Before going inside, he took a final minute to admire the fairyland the ranch had become. At the far end of the pasture twin locust trees looked like white lollipops, the snow-dusted juniper and laurel like a plate of sugar cookies. He wondered if he dared awaken Jane to go for a walk.

The house felt warm after the brisk winter air. Brady made his way through the kitchen and on back to their bedroom. Since their main home in San Antonio had been mostly her creation, Jane had left the ranch house almost untouched. It was their weekend retreat. Except for a few additions, "for the sake of comfort," as Jane put it, the place remained as it had been before. She had wanted it that way as much as he—a place that reflected him, a place where he could retreat when he needed to consult with himself as men were wont to do.

Usually Jane and Scotty accompanied him to the ranch, but not always, and never when he wanted to do a little hunting. That was one area where their differing views of the world had not been fully reconciled. But they'd learned to adopt a live-and-let-live approach that served the marriage well. In point of fact, though, he hunted less than he used to, and he had become a patron of the San Antonio Symphony—something more than one San Antonian had never thought they'd see.

The reason hadn't been Jane so much as his change of fortune in the oil business. The new horizontal drilling technique the engineers had developed had worked big time on his last lease down in the Austin Chalk. A year to the day following their wedding, his gusher had come in, spewing Coleman money all over south Texas.

That night they'd had a magnum of champagne, knowing they had double cause for celebration. After they'd made love he'd whispered in Jane's ear, "How are you going to top this for our second anniversary, darlin'?"

"The question is how *you're* going to top it, Brady," she'd replied.

But damned if they—or Jane, more specifically—hadn't topped it. Scotty was born at one in the morning on their second anniversary. Never had a man been so blessed. A beautiful wife and a son. Brady, who made a point of taking nothing for granted, had vowed to love them both every minute of his life.

"How's the mare doing?" Jane asked as he undressed in the semidarkness of their bedroom.

"Sorry, did I wake you, sugar?"

"No, I've just been dozing, half-awake since you got up."

"Guess what?" he said, as he pulled off his pants.

"What?"

"It snowed last night. And a few flakes are still fallin'."

"Really?"

"Yep. It's beautiful out." Brady pulled back the covers and climbed in beside her.

"Oh, God!" she shrieked, when he snuggled up against her. "You're like a block of ice!"

"How about you warmin' me up a little, Miss Hotpants?"

Jane hooted as he grabbed her, wrapping his arm around her slender waist. She squealed and slithered out of his grasp and out of the bed. "You warm yourself up while I go to the bathroom, Mr. Coleman," she admonished.

Jane trotted off to the bathroom. He admired her nude body until she'd disappeared from sight. Then he eased back on his pillow, savoring the warmth of the bed, and sighed with contentment. How could a man be this happy?

In a few minutes Jane returned. Instead of getting right into bed, she went to the window and pulled back the curtains.

"Oh!" she exclaimed, wrapping her arms around her. "It *is* beautiful!"

"I thought after breakfast I'd take Scotty out to make a snowman."

"He'll have a ball." Jane turned from the window and jumped under the covers. She was chilled herself and snuggled right up to him, finding him more approachable than before. She rubbed his chest and kissed his chin.

Brady turned his head, inhaling her scent. Just the smell of her aroused him. It didn't matter when or where. They could be in an elevator or her office or sitting in an airplane, and an overwhelming urge for her would strike him.

He vigorously rubbed his hand on his stomach to warm his palm. Then he cupped her breast. "I was thinking of askin' if you wanted to go for a walk in our winter wonderland out there."

"It's so pretty, I'd enjoy that."

He ran his hand over her stomach, savoring the suppleness of her skin. " 'Course, that was before I got in bed and discovered this irresistible little creature beside me," he purred.

Jane turned her mouth up and he kissed it, relishing the taste of it. Already he was becoming aroused.

"You keep this up and you're going to melt all the snow single-handedly," she murmured, taking his swollen sex in her cool hand.

"I suppose there are worse ways to spend a snowy morn," he replied.

Jane pulled him over on top of her and they kissed again. She opened her legs and his hips settled between them. He could feel her warm, moist opening. She reached down with her hand and guided him into her. They both groaned with pleasure at their union.

He kissed the corner of her mouth. "That was a pretty brief overture, wasn't it, darlin'?"

"*You're* the patron," she cooed.

"Of the symphony, not the opera."

Jane smiled into his eyes. "Maybe I should sign you up for the opera, too."

"Darlin', there's only one kind of music I'm interested in makin' right now."

She took his face in her hands and kissed him deeply. "Then let's hear it, maestro," she said.

They made love with energy. It wasn't always that way—sometimes it was very slow and with great tenderness. Jane told him early on that she liked variety in lovemaking. "I can be many different women," she'd said, "depending on my mood." He told her that sounded good to him. "It had better," she'd warned, "because it's the only variety you'll ever get!"

That had been fine with him. Dr. Jane Stewart—she'd kept her professional name for work—was the only woman he'd ever want or need. With her in his life, there was no room for anyone else.

They were both getting excited and moving to climax. Brady knew her so well he could anticipate her every desire. Yet in other aspects of their life, she could surprise him. Like that day during their engagement when she'd met him at the airport in San Francisco after he'd been on a two-week business trip to Texas. There she was on her own two feet—no wheelchair, no walker, no cane. They'd spent that afternoon celebrating in a suite she'd rented at the Fairmont Hotel.

"Oh, Brady," she begged, "I want to be on top."

They rolled over and she sat up on him, riding him, her full breasts bobbing above him in the muted light of dawn. "I can't wait much longer," he gasped, feeling the storm building in his loins.

"Now, then!" she cried. "Now!"

They came together, putting his old bed through one hell of a ride. Finally she collapsed on him, her breasts feeling as cool as ice cream on a summer day. But her breath was hot and it seared his skin. She ran her tongue around the shell of his ear.

"I love you, cowboy," she whispered. "Damned if I don't."

"Not half so much as I love you, darlin'."

She lifted her head. "Now, how would you know?"

"A man who works around animals like I do understands the female mind, believe me."

Jane gave him a poke and rolled down beside him. Just then Scotty cried in the next room.

"Well," Jane said, sounding like she was not at all surprised, "I believe our day has begun."

"His timing is pretty good, you've got to admit."

"He's *your* son, Brady."

He laughed. "Whose turn to get him?"

"Yours."

"Seems to me you said that yesterday mornin', too."

"I did," she confessed. "But it's still your turn."

"That's what I like about you doctors—you're so logical."

"Go on, Brady," she said, giving him a shove. "You just had the best sex of your life . . . or at least the best you'll get today."

He went off to the baby's room, returning a minute later with their little romper-clad bundle of joy. He put Scotty next to Jane and climbed back in bed so that the baby was between them.

The toddler prattled on contentedly, happy to be where he liked it best. Jane kissed him and smiled at Brady, her eyes shimmering.

"What's that happy glow all about, missy?" he asked. "You haven't been playin' out behind the barn with the boys, have you?"

"As a matter of fact, I have."

"Oh?"

"But that's not what the glow's all about."

Brady gave her a questioning look.

"Actually," she said, "maybe it *is* what the glow's about."

He gave her a quizzical look.

"I've got news," she said. "I was planning on saving it until Saturday when we go to your mother's for dinner, but since I've got both my men here, and it's a lovely snowy day, I might as well tell you now."

"Tell us what?"

She reached over and took his hand. "There's going to be another baby in the family."

"What?"

She nodded. "I tested myself twice to be sure."

Brady's jaw dropped, his eyes widening with surprise. "Jane! Really?"

"Yep."

He reached over and gave her a big kiss, making Scotty squawk.

"Don't you go gettin' jealous just yet, partner," Brady said, tapping his son's nose.

Brady looked back at Jane. Her eyes were shining.

"Maybe this time it will be a Leigh," she said.

Brady's eyes filled. "Maybe, but it's fine if it's not."

"I know you'd love another little boy just as much," she said, "but for your sake I hope you get your little girl."

He looked out the window. Leigh's kisses were still drifting down from heaven. He didn't say anything, but he had a hunch that this time he would be getting his little girl. Fate, he'd discovered, did work in mysterious, magical ways. Damn, but life was great.

HARLEQUIN
Temptation®

COMING NEXT MONTH

Take 4 bestselling love stories FREE

Plus get a FREE surprise gift!

Special Limited-time Offer

Mail to Harlequin Reader Service®

3010 Walden Avenue
P.O. Box 1867
Buffalo, N.Y. 14269-1867

YES! Please send me 4 free Harlequin Temptation® novels and my free surprise gift. Then send me 4 brand-new novels every month, which I will receive before they appear in bookstores. Bill me at the low price of $2.66 each plus 25¢ delivery and applicable sales tax, if any.* That's the complete price and a savings of over 10% off the cover prices—quite a bargain! I understand that accepting the books and gift places me under no obligation ever to buy any books. I can always return a shipment and cancel at any time. Even if I never buy another book from Harlequin, the 4 free books and the surprise gift are mine to keep forever.

142 BPA AW8V

Name	(PLEASE PRINT)	
Address		Apt. No.
City	State	Zip

This offer is limited to one order per household and not valid to present Harlequin Temptation® subscribers. *Terms and prices are subject to change without notice. Sales tax applicable in N.Y.

UTEMP-895

©1990 Harlequin Enterprises Limited

HARLEQUIN®

Temptation

Secret Fantasies

Do you have a secret fantasy?

Researcher Eva Campbell does. She's an expert on virtual reality and in her computer she's created the perfect man. Except her fantasy lover is much more real than she could ever imagine.... Experience love with the ideal man in Mallory Rush's #558 KISS OF THE BEAST, available in October.

Everybody has a secret fantasy. And you'll find them all in Temptation's exciting new yearlong miniseries, Secret Fantasies. Throughout 1995 one book each month focuses on the hero or heroine's innermost romantic desires....

MOVE OVER, MELROSE PLACE!

> Apartment for rent
> One bedroom
> Bachelor Arms
> 555-1234

Come live and love in L.A. with the tenants of Bachelor Arms. Enjoy a year's worth of wonderful love stories and meet colorful neighbors you'll bump into again and again.

Startling events from Bachelor Arms' past return to stir up scandal, heartache and painful memories for three of its tenants. Read popular Candace Schuler's three sexy and exciting books to find out how passion, love and betrayal at Bachelor Arms affect the lives of three dynamic men. Bestselling author of over fifteen romance novels, Candace is sure to keep you hooked on Bachelor Arms with her steamy, sensual stories.

LOVERS AND STRANGERS #549 (August 1995)

SEDUCED AND BETRAYED #553 (September 1995)

PASSION AND SCANDAL #557 (October 1995)

Next to move into Bachelor Arms are the heroes and heroines in books by ever-popular Judith Arnold!

Don't miss the goings-on at Bachelor Arms

Become a Privileged Woman,
You'll be entitled to all these Free Benefits. And Free Gifts, too.

To thank you for buying our books, we've designed an exclusive FREE program called *PAGES & PRIVILEGES™*. You can enroll with just one Proof of Purchase, and get the kind of luxuries that, until now, you could only read about.

BIG HOTEL DISCOUNTS

A privileged woman stays in the finest hotels. And so can you—at up to 60% off! Imagine standing in a hotel check-in line and watching as the guest in front of you pays $150 for the same room that's only costing you $60. Your *Pages & Privileges* discounts are good at Sheraton, Marriott, Best Western, Hyatt and thousands of other fine hotels all over the U.S., Canada and Europe.

FREE DISCOUNT TRAVEL SERVICE

A privileged woman is always jetting to romantic places.

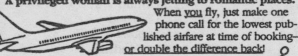

When you fly, just make one phone call for the lowest published airfare at time of booking— or double the difference back!

PLUS—you'll get a $25 voucher to use the first time you book a flight AND 5% cash back on every ticket you buy thereafter through the travel service!